IF YOU ONLY BELIEVE

IF YOU ONLY BELIEVE

❀

A Blessed Collection of Spiritual Tales

Violet E. Holland

Writers Club Press
New York Lincoln Shanghai

If You Only Believe
A Blessed Collection of Spiritual Tales

Writers Club Press
an imprint of iUniverse, Inc.

For information address:
iUniverse, Inc.
2021 Pine Lake Road, Suite 100
Lincoln, NE 68512
www.iuniverse.com

ISBN: 0-595-25656-2

Printed in the United States of America

To Adam and Kaylee May the love that began your lives and encircles you now be passed along life's way to all those you encounter.
Love, Ganny

Contents

❀

Acknowledgements

❀

All the glory goes to God. A great appreciation and respect goes to my husband, Michael, who always gave me the confidence I needed to write. My children, Chasity, Hope, Rocky and Zachary who inspired me to create these images of love, and to all of my many friends who loved me in spite of myself. Lillian Sterling, my fourth grade teacher, who started me on this path, and Pastor Zack Finch who taught me what I needed to know, and to Calvary Baptist Church for welcoming me into their family. And last but not least, to my internet friends who woke with me in the morning and cared enough to ask.

Miss Emily Waters

I remember the way she held her head when she laughed. A little tilted with a one-sided smile that could not be mimicked if one tried. Her eyes were bright, and she never let things get her down. When asked by some what her secret was, she would just give that beautiful smile a full workout and reply, '*To know me is to love me.*' This would sound like a conceited remark coming from most people, but not from her. You would believe it just by the innocence of her smile. I never heard anyone say anything about her that was not positive or complimentary. She was the town angel.

I'll never forget the day she left this earth to go meet our heavenly Father. It was a day of sadness that filled the whole town with sorrow. She had given her life for what she believed and she will always be remembered for the wonderful deeds that she has done.

Emily grew up on the poor side of town. She came from a rather large family and was not taken care of properly by today's standards. But back then, she had all the things that she needed, and that was enough. Her family was rather ordinary, to say the least, but she seemed to bring out the best in everyone, even as a child. I remember once when old Charlie Borden saw her in the five-and-dime as he chewed his wad of tobacco. He sneered at her as he did all children he encountered, and she just smiled and said, "What nice teeth you have, Mr. Borden." You could hear a pin drop in that room for what seemed like hours (because old Charlie's teeth were as rotten as road-kill after three days), and then old Charlie burst out laughing with a howl that could have awakened the dead. Tilly Piper, the storeowner, put the story fast into motion, and before you knew it Emily Waters was a saint in the eyes of the townspeople and the whole town looked upon her with admiration.

You could oftentimes see Emily helping old ladies to the grocery store or watching young children for free while their poor mothers worked to try and make ends meet. The local church eventually hired her as the secretary because Preacher Tom said that the Lord intended for her to be there. It was quite surprising because the town church had never had a secretary before, and she was *so young.* Her age never seemed to stop her from doing what she felt needed to be done, though. Emily would get up at the break of dawn and meet with the children of Millsboro just so they could pray before school. Each child would leave the church with a large grin on his or her face and even seemed to listen better to Miss Polly, the schoolteacher at school when they arrived. No one knew what she was saying to those children when she had them inside, but no one ever questioned it. Emily was blessed and the whole town knew it.

It was on a Friday when it all happened. She was walking home from church when she saw a fight break out in front of the old saloon. It was only natural for Emily to step in and try to make peace. Conroy Reed, the old town drunk, had found him someone he could ruffle the feathers of. It seemed a drifter was just passing through and had gotten into a game of poker with old Conroy. Apparently he was losing when he decided to *take it outside.* Emily ran towards them with her bright pink dress fluttering in the wind, softly calling out that God loved them and would not approve of their behavior. I'll never forget the scream that filled the air when the drifter pulled a hunting knife out of his boot and began to slash old Conroy. Emily stepped right into the middle of it without the slightest glimpse of fear. The drifter boy was wielding the knife to and fro in such a fit that it took Sheriff Abe and a loaded shotgun to get him to lay it down.

After Sheriff Abe had gotten the drifter to lie down on the ground and had cuffed him, the people on the street all ran towards Emily whose soft pink dress was now mostly crimson. There were wails of grief throughout Main Street that day—and many more at the funeral.

You probably think that that's the end of her story, don't you? Well, sit tight because I'm just beginning the story. The things that happened in Millsboro after that are too peculiar for you to believe unless you were there both before and after. The next Tuesday morning when the children started back to school (Monday school was closed so all of the children could be at Emily's funeral), they all marched right into the church just as if they were expecting to see Miss Emily standing there waiting for them. The time they spent inside the church was the same amount of time that Emily would have kept them. They marched out single file with smiles on each and every face and walked straight to school whistling "The Old Rugged Cross."

Now, some of the townsfolk started talking about how they didn't think it was too healthy for those children to be still meeting like that. So they took their complaints over to Preacher Tom and laid them out for him. Preacher Tom would only say that he "won't turning no children out of his church no matter what time of day it was or what reason." As far as old Preacher Tom was concerned, those children could meet there everyday for the rest of their lives. Even the parents were curious as to why those little children went to the church even after Miss Emily had passed on. They would question their children and get answers that they couldn't argue with. Since none of the parents thought there was any harm in children going to church, they refused to stop them.

It was about two weeks after Miss Emily's funeral that those children started to gather on Saturdays to help little old ladies cross streets and carry groceries out. They all got together the following week and placed a cross out front of the old church with a thorn wreath at the very top. Willard Reeves, the local carpenter, saw them out there struggling with it, so he stopped to help them get it into the ground. It was quite pretty to look at, and the whole town had stories going as to why that old cross was put up. But the truth of the matter is that no one knew why those children had put up the cross.

Those children didn't stop there, either. Nope. It was several Saturdays later that we saw them out there whistling to "Sweet Chariot" and painting the old church white—a color the church hadn't seen in quite some time. There was no mistaking that those kids were moved by something Miss Emily had shared with them. The work that they did seemed to touch the hearts of the whole town. It wasn't any time before they had twenty adults out there in the churchyard whistling and working with them. Everybody was doing his own little thing to make the church look new. I couldn't help myself but to go out there and help too, and the funniest thing happened. I found myself whistling a tune that I never even knew that I knew. "When The Roll Is Called Up Yonder" came flowing out my mouth like there was no tomorrow. And you know what else? I never felt so good in my life.

It took about three Saturdays before the church was finished, and before we could rest in the sun those children were at it again. That's right. Old Miss Hattie Brooks had been a widow for fourteen years, and her place looked like it. Those children showed up early one Saturday morning with mowers and rakes and flower seeds—just about anything you can think of. And it wasn't long before the adults were out there helping again. Everybody was out there whistling and smiling like they were drunk on some good cider, but they hadn't touched a thing. I'll never forget it, not for as long as I live.

This Good Samaritan behavior kept up throughout the whole summer. It looked as though the entire town was getting a make-over—and all because a bunch of children got it started. Then fall set in, and we all thought that whatever had gotten into those children would disappear. We soon found out how wrong we were. It was nearing Thanksgiving when the children placed a sign out by the road that said *Thanksgiving Feast, Please come eat with us this year! All meals brought will be gladly appreciated.* Well, I guess you must know that everybody in the whole town showed up for this wonderful feast. And wonderful it was. The poor were blessed with fine food, and the rich were blessed with unconditional love. Those children had done it again.

Preacher Tom took the opportunity to share the Word of God with everyone and to remind them that they didn't have to wait for an invitation to come back again, because the door was always open. The children all waited for the adults to eat, and then they served themselves and huddled in a corner off to the side. Nobody bothered them. We just had a feeling that their little minds were working on the next event that they had in store for the town, and we really seemed to like everything that they had managed so far. The people of Millsboro left talking and laughing with one another like no one had ever seen before. There was Mayor Cecil Givens who was talking with old farmer Bart Jones like they had been friends all their lives. And even the Mayor's wife invited Bart's wife Freda to her next party. I'd never seen anything like it in all my life.

The Saturday following the Thanksgiving Feast we saw the children hauling in a huge cedar that had been given to them by old Bart Jones. They worked on that tree from dawn until dusk, and it was the prettiest tree I ever laid my eyes on. The lights came on right around dark, and they lit up the entire churchyard. There just seemed to be no end to what those little people could do.

The following Saturday a new sign went up and this one said, *Christmas Celebration! Come one Come all. Come see what it's all about!* Well, that got the whole town talking, and some were planning on coming just to see what it was all about. Throughout those next weeks, we watched the children carrying in box after box of materials unknown to anyone but themselves. Excitement was in the air! Adults were talking about the surprise evening at church like children waiting on Santa.

Mayor Cecil's wife, Martha, started calling all of her bridge and tea party associates and asked them to help cook a gigantic dinner for the town of Millsboro to be eaten before the wonderful celebration that would take place that evening. I've never seen ladies humming around town like that in all the years that I've lived here (and that's been seventy-two years this March). Tilly Piper had to order twice the usual that year for the store. She said she had never sold so much food since she'd opened the doors. And while all the ladies of Millsboro were preparing for the feast, all the townsmen got together and started building the nativity scene to place outside the front of the church just below the children's cross. It seemed that the whole town had somehow been touched by the love of poor Emily Waters.

The next morning just before sunup, we awoke to see a large star standing over the cross. Its light was beaming down perfectly on the nativity scene. It almost looked as though the North Star had swooped down from the sky and landed right over our little church of Millsboro. Those children had been at it again. The town was starting to wonder if they ever got any sleep at night.

Well, it wasn't long before the great event arrived. Main Street was lined with cars as far as the eyes could see. I seem to recall that folks from other towns were coming to see what this great event was all about. Ladies were walking back and forth from their cars toting turkeys and casserole dishes like there was no tomorrow. The men were setting up tables wherever they could find a place to put them. The children were nowhere to be seen, but we all knew they were close by preparing their great event.

Preacher Tom started the dinner off with a wonderful prayer that mentioned the name of Emily Waters and praised her for all of her wonderful work at the church, both before and after her death. The children stepped out from the sanctuary and offered to help serve the food so that the ladies could eat with their husbands for the blessed event. The ladies were all charmed that these children could be so kind as to make such an offer, and then they took them up on it. After everyone was served, the children filled their plates and headed back to the sanctuary. Only Stanley Finch remained by the tables. The tall lanky fellow gently took a spoon and tapped it lightly on one of the glass serving dishes.

"May I have your attention, please," he asked as though he wasn't sure what he was going to say next.

The whole room, which had been filled with a mixture of laughter and conversation, became silent. The townspeople all turned their heads toward Stanley and watched silently as they waited for him to speak.

"I would like for everyone to meet in the church sanctuary by 7:00, at which time we will share with you why you were invited here for our celebration this year. I'll see you soon." And with that he walked towards the door that led to the room with the many wooden pews.

The room again filled with a loud din of conversation. Mostly curiosity questions like 'What do you think those children have planned?' or "What do you suppose those children are up to now?' It wouldn't be long before they would find out.

At about quarter to seven, the congregation of folks began to walk towards the door that would carry them into the church's sanctuary. Their eyes lit up with amazement as they headed towards the pews to find a seat. Glass stars hung from the ceiling that glistened with many colors from the Christmas tree that was so well lit. But right in the middle of the ceiling was a large star shining like it had been pulled from the sky itself, and right in the center of it was a picture of the beautiful Emily Waters. There was a silence of complete awe surrounding the room. All you could here was the shuffling of feet as the people tried to make their way to a seat. The pews filled in no time, and the walls began to support others who would rather stand than miss the special event unfolding that night.

Pretty little Marla Dobbs with her golden curls was standing behind the altar, patiently waiting for everyone to quiet down. Then she began.

"I would like to thank everyone for coming here this evening. We would first like to sing some Christmas carols so we don't forget why we celebrate this blessed day, and then we would like to tell you what this evening is all about. So let's please start by singing "O Little Town of Bethlehem." The joyous singing that night was like nothing anyone could ever imagine. It sounded like the biggest choir in the world. No one was holding back. They were singing like there was no tomorrow. It almost seemed as though God's angels had joined in on our praises. We continued to sing the Christmas carols that are so loved by everyone, and each one sounded as good as the first. And finally the time had arrived for those children to tell us *what it was all about.*

The crowd sat and watched silently as about twenty-five children walked up to the altar and stood behind Stanley Finch and Marla Dobbs who were the oldest of the group. Stanley pulled out a sheet of paper from his pocket and looked down at it. His dark eyes began to mist over with tears, and then he looked up at the crowd and balled the paper up in his hand. He stepped up to the podium and began, "I had a nice proper speech written for this occasion, but I think that what I have to say I can say without help."

"Miss Emily brought us here each and every day to tell us just how special we were. She told us that we were loved and that we would never be alone. And when Miss Emily passed away, we were all afraid that we would not be loved any longer. So we talked about it at Miss Emily's funeral and decided that we would continue to meet here and love one another. We would take out our Bibles and read scriptures just like Miss Emily would have us do. As we read each day, we realized that Miss Emily wasn't the only one who loved us. What she had been telling us was that God loved us also, and He wanted us to love one another. We prayed to God and asked Him to bring Miss

Emily back to us. As you all well know, He didn't. Then Marla had a dream and came to school and shared it with us, and now she'd like to share it with you."

He paused and looked behind him, calling, "Marla."

Marla stepped up to the podium. Her frail body visibly displayed the constant battle she fought with arthritis. Her dark hair accented the dark rings under her eyes, and the wrenching of her hands was typical. "In my dream," she said, "God was a radiant beam of light. And He whispered to me that Miss Emily was not dead and that she lived where there was peace and beauty all around her. The only way we could have Miss Emily back was by finding out what Miss Emily wanted us to know. So that is what we did. At first we thought she would come walking back into the church at any time, but as we continued to do the things that Miss Emily had taught us, we realized that Miss Emily is alive in each and every one of us. You see, Miss Emily took the time to show us how to feel good about ourselves, and she taught us that we all have a purpose.

"She taught us that love lives inside of us, and if we live the way our Bible instructs us to, we will someday be with her again holding hands and walking among the streets of gold that we know she has already walked on. We want to finish her message since she didn't get to live long enough to share it with you. It's all about love, and we want you to know so you can tell your friends and they can tell theirs. God asked us to spread the Word and somehow the world just got to busy to do that."

Marla stepped back, and Stanley stepped back up to the podium. He wiped the beads of perspiration off his forehead and softly said, "Miss Emily wanted the world to love one another, and so does God. She died before she could see our little town helping one another like they did this summer, but she didn't die in vain. We can show God and Miss Emily that we haven't forgotten what it's all about just by what we have been doing and will keep on doing.

"So Marla and I and all the other kids up here would like for you to stop calling us *those children* and refer to us as *God's children* 'cause that's what it's all about."

He wiped a small tear from his eye and wrestled with the next words.

"Thank you all for coming and don't let Miss Emily fade away."

The pews were silent for the longest minute in the world, and then people started clapping and then standing. Others were screaming "BRAVO." The evening ended with each person walking up to God's children and shaking their hands, offering to help with supplies, labor and money. The outpouring was wonderful. The event had such an effect on the town that afterwards we built up and repaired everything we could get our hands on in Millsboro. Then we hit the next little town of Dagsboro, and I'm sure we'll continue on as long as it's the Lord's will. Each project begins with the song "Amazing Grace," and throughout the day, whistling tunes of favorite hymns can be heard from far off.

Miss Emily Waters may not be here to see it, but I'm sure God is telling her everything that took place down here. And she's probably sitting somewhere on a beautiful glass star way up in heaven waiting for *God's children* to arrive.

Ole Wooly

I could never forget that old man or the way people looked up to him. It wasn't like he was an important politician or even a local businessman. In fact, he was an old bum, but the tattered clothing that he wore was always clean. I never saw him wear any shoes other than those that I first saw him in when I was six years old. They were the kind that you saw the old farmers clean their stalls out with. I think they call them combat boots today. The stubble on his face was there more often than not. But it was that old blazer he wore that earned him his name.

It didn't matter if it was a hundred degrees outside—he always had that old wool jacket on. *Ole Wooly* was his pet name around town, and he seemed to like the title. People around town said he was a messenger, blessed with a heart of gold that seemed to touch many. Although one might think that he was startling to look at, to say the least, everyone in town had an eerie sort of love for him.

There were lots of stories around town that described the many good deeds that Ole Wooly had done throughout his long life. There seemed to be no end to what he was capable of. It wasn't just his helpfulness that made him special, however; it was the luck that seemed to follow him wherever he would go. Peter Spencer, the local grocer, often told the story of how Ole Wooly had been present when two young thugs had walked into the grocery store and tried to rob him. He says that Ole Wooly walked up behind them and started chanting, "Lord, forgive these two boys here and teach them the power of your Word so they walk in evil no more." The oldest one, who was toting the gun, turned around and shot Ole Wooly in the blink of an eye. Ole Wooly fell back against the candy rack, clutching at his chest, and Peter says he thought that that was the end of him right there.

But Ole Wooly surprised everyone when he stood up and looked those boys in the eyes and asked, "Now do you believe the power of the Lord is greater than you?"

The boys are said to have dropped the gun and thrown up their hands in total disbelief. When Sheriff Joe arrived, those boys were on their knees crying and asking the Lord to forgive them. Sheriff Joe said that it was like nothing he had ever seen in his life.

After the boys were hauled off to the old county jail, Peter asked Ole Wooly how he had managed to walk away from a gunshot wound. Ole Wooly gave that sideways grin that oftentimes seemed quite crazy and pulled an old Gideon Bible from out of his wool jacket. Then he replied, "The Lord took that bullet for me." And sure enough, there was a bullet lodged in the center of the small brown Bible Ole Wooly toted around in his pocket. When he opened the book, the lead from the bullet fell on the countertop still intact. Peter shared his story with anyone who would listen to it, and before you knew it people were calling him a messenger sent from the Heavens above.

It wasn't long after that that Viola Parker, the widow from Millsboro, told Bessie Jones that she had been sitting on the bridge thinking about jumping off when Ole Wooly had appeared from out of nowhere. According to her, he had no way of knowing what her intentions were, but he just started talking about what would happen to anyone crazy enough to jump off. She claims that none of that really seemed to matter to her until she looked down and the rippling waters below were no longer there. She claims that she saw a fire below her that had arms stretched out towards her that were charred and mangled. She swears she even felt heat on her face, and there is no convincing her that she didn't see what she says she saw.

The story has it that Ole Wooly walked away without looking back, and Viola waited until he was gone before changing her mind and deciding that life was worth living after all.

I don't know how true those stories are, but I do know that my own is as true as the old oak that sits in front of the old courthouse. I haven't shared it with many folk because sometimes I have a hard time believing it myself. I was fifteen the day that Ole Wooly made his appearance in my life, and I'll tell you right now that I have been a changed man ever since. Tommy Dobbs and I had decided to take his papa's boat one Monday right after school had let out in June. Of course we had been told many times not to take out the boat, and we had always listened. But on that particular Monday we were up to no good, and we had our minds made up. The intention was to carry the boat across the river where Heidi Stover lived and to show off a little bit for her. Tommy had had a crush on her for a year, and when school let out for the summer, he still hadn't had enough courage to carry her books home for her. That day he was feeling a little brave, and I was always looking for excitement.

It took forever for us to shove the old boat off the shore and get it sitting pretty along the water's edge. Determination goes a long way, though and when Tommy thought of Heidi in her pretty long curls he couldn't help but shove that thing with every ounce of strength he had. And before you knew it, we were in the little boat paddling towards the home of Heidi Stover.

I took out of my sock one of the Camel cigarettes I had taken from Dad and offered Tommy one. There we were, the both of us sitting back in the old boat puffing on cigarettes like we were a couple of old retirees out for a day of relaxation. Then out of the corner of my eye, I saw him. It was Ole Wooly standing on the shore and shaking his head in disapproval. I sat up quickly and tossed the cigarette into the water.

"Did you see that?" I asked Tommy.

"See what?" was his reply as he puffed franticly on his own Camel.

"Did you just see Ole Wooly over there shaking his head at us?"

Tommy burst out laughing. "There's no way you saw Ole Wooly over there. Them woods there are as thick as they were when the pilgrims landed here. That there is Pops Spicer's land, and it ain't been walked on since he bought the place. Besides, Ole Wooly wouldn't risk Pop's shotgun. I don't care what kind of messenger he is."

He was right. Pops had more *No Trespassing* signs on that property than Farmer Brooks had beans in his garden. Still, I couldn't shake the feeling. I was sure I had seen Ole Wooly standing there on the shore.

We paddled on past the old bridge that joined the two sides of Millsboro and headed out towards the opening at the river, and it was there that I heard Ole Wooly just as plain as day.

"You must turn back now."

Tommy jerked his head up from paddling and looked around with a confused look on his face. I was relieved to see that I wasn't the only one who heard him.

"Do you reckon that old man is trying to scare us or something?" he asked with a look of concern.

"Naw, that's not Ole Wooly's way, you know. He preaches the Word too much to be out to terrorize a couple of kids. Maybe it's just the wind. It seems to be picking up right now. And it looks as though it's getting dark a little earlier than usual, too," I said, trying to sound as confidant as possible but certain I hadn't been successful.

"Well, Ole Wooly can do what he wants, but I didn't risk a tanning of my hide for nothing, and I'm gonna see Heidi even if it's for a split second. I just want to wave and let her see that she ain't lookin' at no boy here."

He flexed the muscle of his right arm as he spoke. We laughed at the sight of his wimpy little arms that had not formed yet into a young man's but were awkwardly heading towards that day.

We were just coasting towards the creek when I saw the first bolt of lightning and realized that the sun was not going down early, but rather a storm had started to roll in. I started to get this feeling that we should have listened to the voice of Ole Wooly. Perhaps he knew there was danger ahead, and in some miraculous kind of way he had let us know. I was no longer enjoying the ride but wishing that I were at home in the barn nestled on some hay reading a *National Geographic* and smoking one of my dad's Camels.

Tommy looked up at the sky and said, "I think we may have to ask the damsel for some shelter, matey. Certainly she wouldn't leave two soldiers of love out to the mercy of Mother Nature's wrath, would she?"

He cackled with excitement. There was no turning Tommy back now. He was on a mission and had his mind set on seeing Heidi Stover. The wind had begun to howl a little, and the warm air that had been bringing beads of perspiration to our foreheads was gone. The cool wind that whipped all around us was arousing a fear inside of me, and all that I could think was how desperately I wanted to go back home. There was a loud burst of lightening and…*one-one thousand, two-one thousand, three-one thousand, four-one thousand*…the sound of thunder roared through the air as if to say this was the real thing. Then a bolt of lightning struck something in the distance. The storm was only a few miles away. There was no way that Tommy and I could make it back home safely. We had to seek some sort of shelter, and we had to do it fast!

It was then that the rain began to pelt down on us, drenching our clothes within seconds. My heart was racing, and I was looking all around for some little cove we could paddle our way into when I saw Ole Wooly again. He was waving his hand back and forth as though he were telling us to come towards him. How could Ole Wooly be in so many places along the shore? It is a question I still ask myself today.

"Tommy, we have to head the boat down there!" I screamed as I pointed towards the shore where I saw Ole Wooly standing.

"No way! Heidi is having us over for dinner, and she's got a snug little blanket she wants to wrap me up in and sit me in front of her fireplace," he yelled back with a grin that sent shivers through my spine.

I turned and looked down the cove as we floated past it. Ole Wooly was holding up a sign on which was written *Psalm 23*. I thought the old man was losing it. Why anyone would be standing on the shore with a sign in his hand like that in this kind of weather was beyond me. I looked back to see if perhaps I was mistaken, and when I did he was gone. I rubbed my eyes and looked back once again. He was gone, or maybe he had never been there.

The lightning struck again, and this time the thunder was right behind it. It was here! The storm was right over us, and we were sitting right smack in the middle of a creek—the worst place one could be in a storm. I could see the lights of Heidi Stover's house burning faintly from a distance. It wasn't that far, but it seemed like miles. Then the lightning struck, hitting the water beside the small boat we were seated in. The heat from the closeness of the strike went through my body, and my hair stood on its ends. We were going to die out here, and I was helpless to do anything about it.

I could hear Tommy screaming, but I couldn't see him. The evening was dark and the rain was coming down furiously, but he was screaming and I had to find him. He was no longer inside the boat. My body was aching all over, and fear had consumed what was left of me. I closed my eyes and began to cry. The tears and the sobs that were flowing from me were hard to believe they were even coming from me. Then I pictured the sign in my head, as plain as day: Psalm 23, and suddenly I knew what I was supposed to do. I stood in the small boat that was slowly filling up with water, and at the top of my voice I began repeating some of the verse that I had learned in

Bible School. *"Yea, though I walk through the valley of the shadow of death, I shall fear no evil; for thou art with me…"*

The rain began to slow down, and the wind ceased its howling like something from the Twilight Zone. I could see Tommy clutching onto a piece of driftwood that was floating nearby. He was sobbing uncontrollably, and he didn't seem to even know I was still close by.

"Tommy, I'm coming! Don't let go!" I screamed to him as I threw myself into the black water.

Thy rod and thy staff, they comfort me.

I swam as fast as I could. In spite of the darkness, I could see that his eyes were blood red and his skin color was not of this earth. I grabbed his arm and started pulling him towards me. He was sobbing and fighting me, refusing to let go of the driftwood that held him up.

"It's me, Tommy. You have to let go so I can get you to the shore."

Thou preparest a table before me in the presence of mine enemies…

His arms were flying around in all directions, and then they caught my neck and began to tighten firmly. I swam as best I could to get us both to the shore before my strength gave out. My heart was sounding throughout my head, and all that I could hear was the heaving of my own chest. Just a little further…

Surely goodness and mercy shall follow me all the days of my life…

When I reached the shore, I had to lay Tommy on the soft pine needles while I ran toward the Stover's home screaming for help. The door opened, and Mr. Stover stepped out on the porch with his rifle in his hands, looking as though he was not quite sure what to expect. I told him lightning had jolted our boat, and that Tommy was lying in the woods. Mrs. Stover called for help while Heidi and her father ran through the woods to help me find my best friend who was lying somewhere within its darkness.

Tommy got his wish that night. Heidi wrapped him up in a blanket while we waited in front of the fireplace for the ambulance to arrive. He was in shock and was suffering from burns from the light-ening that had almost struck him, but he was going to be all right.

I waited for my father to come pick me up, and I remember little else.

…and I will dwell in the house of the Lord forever and ever. Amen.

I'm sure I got a nice long lecture on the way home, but all I could think of was Ole Wooly and the sign that he had held there on the shore. I knew that God had put him there, and I knew that no one would believe me if I told them about it. So I just closed my eyes and thanked God for helping me get through the most frightening experience of my life. I was safe and so was Tommy, thanks to God's messenger.

Yesterday I went to Ole Wooly's funeral. His old heart finally stopped beating. I was amazed at the outpouring of people who came to say goodbye to the town bum. Hugh Williams, the town mayor, stood beside his wife, Mabel, as she wept. Joe Barnes, the town banker, and all of his clerks were there. The whole Ruritan Club, the Ladies Auxiliary, and even the school band had come to say a farewell to Ole Wooly.

Just moments after the preacher was through eulogizing and had finished his prayer, the sun peeked out from around the cloud-filled sky, and a dozen doves flew down towards the coffin that held the remains of Ole Wooly. Such brightness filled the sky that it brought a temporary blindness to all those looking on. When we could all see again, the doves were gone and the heavens seemed very much at peace. I don't know what happened there yesterday, but I believe God sent those doves down to bring his messenger home.

So if you should happen to pass an old bum on the street, don't think of him too poorly, because he just might be one of God's messengers. Or who knows? It could even be Ole Wooly. After all, when you work for God, nothing's impossible.

The Coming

*T*here were no stars in the sky that night. Although the moon was full, I had never seen it quite so gray. *The world seems considerably darker*, I thought as I sat there on my front porch in the wee hours of the morning. I am an insomniac, so there is nothing peculiar about me sitting on my porch like I was doing that night. I rocked back and forth on the old swing listening to the familiar squeaks that accompanied its motion. Besides the moon looking so dull, that night was no different from any other night that I found myself outside listening to the birds as the world sleeps. Then I watched as a flock of doves flew from out of the trees and straight up into the heavens. It was at that moment that I felt something was different, yet I couldn't quite put my finger on what it was. I had never seen a flock of doves and certainly wouldn't be expecting to see one at such a late hour as this. Then they were gone as quickly as they had appeared.

The wind began to howl as though there were a northeaster blowing in, but I had heard no forecast that predicted such a storm. I just sat there in my swing watching as the wind picked up and carried away pieces of debris that had been left behind by the neighborhood children. The sounds that I heard next were unfamiliar and frightening yet somehow peaceful as well. The howling sounded like a million-man choir that was humming softly into the wind—humming so melodically that I found myself comforted by the sound. The wind had never sounded so peculiar in all my years of sitting awake throughout the night on my old front porch. Peculiar it was and yet quite soothing.

I stood and walked to the edge of the old decaying porch. The wind was brushing up against my face, and the smell in the air was so sweet. I felt a comforting shiver glide slowly up my body, and for a brief second I thought that I was dead and slowly drifting my way up to heaven. I spread my arms out to the side and imagined that I was like one of God's beautiful birds that soar through the sky. Twisting and turning my head with the wind, my body swayed back and forth as though I was in the air and being carried by the wind. And then the night grew light, and the sky was as bright as a fresh new morning. I watched in disbelief as white objects that appeared almost transparent lifted up into the sky. And the humming (it was so sweet) became louder and louder as though someone had turned up the volume.

My legs were locked in place as I watched the most amazing event unfold before my eyes. The wind lavishly brushed my cheeks as I watched a parade of what looked like angels of all sizes glide smoothly towards the sky. I closed my eyes and pulled the fresh air that swirled around me deep into my lung, letting it fill me with the life-giving freshness that warm evenings can offer the soul. A sweet scent of roses was in the air. Then the humming began to mellow out, and the sky began to grow dark again. I opened my eyes just in time to see another flock of doves float past and head straight up into the heavens. Their wings were flapping in the wind as though they were sailing instead of flying. Never have I seen anything like it before.

I should have known that something had happened and even suspected what, but honestly I didn't. The sky had gone back to its usual darkness, and the night became still and quiet. The sweet scent of roses that had filled the air was gone, and all that was left was the warm feeling it had left inside of me. People would never believe this even if I told them about it. I drew in one last deep breath of fresh air, and then I headed inside to try to get a little sleep before morning.

The next morning was typical for an old man. I started my coffeepot and headed into the small dark room where I spent most of my time these last few years, and I turned on the television to hear the local news and weather. I had somehow managed to get plenty of rest the night before and thought I might even take a walk before the traffic got too busy on the old country road I live on. I liked walking in the morning because I felt closer to God then than any at other time of the day. (I knew I didn't pray as much as I should have, but I knew He understood that that's just the way I am). There's a soft mist that hovers over the fields of corn that surround my home, and the birds sing softly as I pass through the silent fields. It's a good way to start every morning.

I switched on the old television that I had been promising I would replace ever since I heard about the new control that lets you change the channel from your chair. An old man like me could certainly appreciate not having to get up from his old lazy boy chair and turn the channel. These last few years my back hasn't been as good as it used to be, and I didn't really expect it to be getting any better. I cautiously sat my old body back down in the worn chair that I so enjoyed taking my afternoon naps in, and I soon recalled all that I had seen this past night.

NEWS FLASH was blinking in large letters across the screen of my old RCA. The pretty brunette on the screen was wearing a face of utter confusion. "This morning thousands of people awoke to find their loved ones missing as if they vanished into thin air," she said. "We have many unconfirmed disappearances that the local sheriff's department and the state police are looking into. It appears that sometime between the hours of midnight and four a.m. the 911 switchboard at the local police department began to light up with calls from frightened family members across the country: people claiming that a family member or members were missing and had left no clue as to where they might have gone. Captain Bill Hayes has asked us to advise all of our viewers to remain calm and to report anything that may have appeared suspicious throughout the night. This is Jan Felderman reporting for WREV. Stay tuned for more information throughout the day. We will keep you informed up to the minute as we receive updates."

I pushed myself up out of the old lazy boy chair I'd been resting in and switched off the television. My legs quivered as I headed toward the kitchen to fix my cup of coffee. *Surely He wouldn't have left me behind.*

I thought of the night before. It almost seemed as if I had dreamed it now. The soft wind and the humming had been real. Could it have been that I had witnessed *the second coming*? I dropped to my knees, and the sobs tore from my lips like the howl of a hungry wolf. He had left me behind, and I was right there watching it all happen.

"Why, God, didn't you take me too?" I screamed up at the ceiling, my heart echoing in my ears while the tears rolled down my cheeks like they had never done before. Not even as a child could I remember feeling so much sorrow and this sense of helplessness all at the same time.

I raised myself up off the floor and poured a cup of coffee. I concentrated on my hand as it shakily emptied the coffee into the cup. There had to be another answer—an answer other than the one I was coming up with. There was no way God would leave me here on this earth with all of those He condemns. *I am a believer!* I screamed inside my head. This cannot be happening, not to me.

I had not always gone to church because I believe you can worship the Lord right at home just as well as in front of a whole lot of people raising their arms and screaming at the heavens. That just isn't my style. I like to worship Him *privately*. Still, He wouldn't leave me behind because of that, would He?

I went back into the small dark living room and sat in my old lazy boy chair. The news flash was still blinking. There were scenes behind the brunette news reporter of people standing in the streets outside of the police department wailing with tears of grief. Some were holding signs that read, *Where are our families?* Or *Do your jobs, locate the lost!* I have never seen such grief in all my life.

Again the tears welled up in my eyes. I knew what had happened last night. Shucks, I had watched it all unfold before me, and I just couldn't believe that He had *forgotten me*. Something wasn't right here. Something just did not make since to me. Hadn't I always helped those I encountered who were in need? And hadn't I always sent my tithes in to old Preacher Tom? None of this was making any sense. Then the thought (it was so loud) came over me, *Good intentions won't get you to heaven*. Was that all it had been—just good intentions?

The brunette on the television began talking about what they were doing to protect the rest of the world that had not been lost throughout the night. "The President has requested that all of the citizens here in the United States go immediately to the nearest government office to be stamped with a special code to prevent any more unexplained disappearances. He states that 'no more of our Country will be abducted by the hands of intruders'. This is a required action that will be followed up on by the local police and government officials." Then the screen flashed to another scene, this one at the town courthouse. There were people pushing their way through the line to get their *stamp* that would protect them from some sort of abduction. I couldn't stand watching any more of this.

I felt my old body slipping from the chair I was sitting in, and I fell to my knees. My hand pushed the on button in, and the screen on the old RCA went black. The tears and sobs were uncontrollable as I clasped my hands together. "My God, why hast Thou forsaken me?" I cried.

And at that moment I felt a warmth come over me—a feeling I have never experienced before in my life. The darkness behind my closed eyes was getting brighter and brighter. I couldn't help but open my eyes to see what was causing such a luminous radiance outside my eyelids. There stood before me the brightest being I have ever laid eyes on. Its arms were outstretched and the light was *so bright!*

"You never accepted Jesus Christ as your Savior. You must accept Him and let Him into your heart, or there will be no chance of ever living eternally."

I stared in disbelief. I could not see the lips of this glorified spirit moving, and yet I knew the words were coming from it. I felt close to heaven, yet so far away all at the same time. I crawled on my knees towards the beautiful light, tears now streaking my face and flowing all the harder.

"I want to come home," I said, "Mary Belle is waiting for me. I've been waiting for twelve years to see her again and to hold her in my arms again. Please help me. Please don't give up on me. I will accept Jesus Christ as my Savior. I always have. I just never knew it was so important that I do it so openly. Please ask God not to forsake me but to give me salvation. I will honor both Him and His wonderful Son, and I will work for the Lord all the days I have left."

I opened my eyes only to find that the light that had filled the room was gone and there was no sign of anything ever having been there. "Oh, God," I cried, "Please hear my pleas. Please give me the chance to prove to You that I am one of Your sheep and I believe, I so strongly believe. Please hear me, Father. Please don't leave me behind!"

There were no signs that I had been heard, just the rickety sounds of my old refrigerator's motor churning in the kitchen, nothing else. I let my body fall forward onto the old musty, Oriental rug that was faded from years of use. The sobs that flowed from my throat were like nothing I had ever heard coming out of myself before.

"Please don't leave me behind, dear Father. Please bring me home."

I sobbed until there was nothing left inside of me. No tears. No feelings. Just complete numbness throughout my body. I had been left behind. There was no eternal life for me. No precious Mary Belle awaiting my entrance through the gates of heaven. Just me, in a world filled with non-believers who were now racing to the government lines for Satan's signature. I pulled myself back into the old lazy boy chair I had spent the past eight years sitting in, and I pulled out the Holy Bible from the end table where it had now gathered so much dust from its lack of use. *Why hadn't I opened it more?* When Mary Belle was alive, she had read it to me every day; and I had listened to the words. I had listened, but I had not obeyed. I thought I knew what I was doing. I thought I had it all figured out.

I opened the old dusty book, and the pages opened to the book of Revelation, chapter twenty-two, and my eyes fell on the final verses: *"And if any man shall take away from the words of the book of this prophecy, God shall take away his part out of the book of life, and out of the holy city, and from the things which are written in this book. He which testifieth these things saith, Surely I come quickly: Amen. Even so, come, Lord Jesus."*

It was then that I felt the first pains in my chest—something that would have scared me so at one time, but this day I welcomed the pain. For I had accepted Jesus, and the glorified Spirit was there. And I knew I was ready. Ready for a long awaited journey where peace awaited me.

"Yes, Jesus, please come take my weary soul."

The pain keeps getting stronger and the peace keeps following behind. I am leaving, I'm going to see Mary Belle. Once again, I'll see my precious Mary Belle.

"The grace of our Lord Jesus Christ be with you all. Amen."

Land of Believe

The simple notion of what's right and what's wrong can be so complex for some. I myself struggle with it from time to time. Seems like there is no perfect way of living here on this earth. I do believe, however, that there's a world out there where bountiful love exists and the people's hearts are filled with good intentions. I even believe that I visited there once. It was about two years ago on a beautiful summer day when I had been walking for hours. I have always been one to enjoy clean fresh air and the warmth of sunlight on my skin, and that day had been particularly pleasant.

I live out in the country and don't have to worry much with fast cars and noisy backfiring. There are no crazy drivers blowing me off the road as they whiz by, and strangers are few and far between. I had found myself about eight miles away from home on an old back road when I saw a dirt road in the middle of a wooded lot. As you probably already know, dirt roads are not uncommon out in the country. But you don't usually see them in the middle of a wooded lot where the ditch is overgrown with grass and where scraps of debris from years past lays on top of them. I wondered why the road was so neatly pruned and while the trench that blocked its entrance had not been so much as mowed. Who could possibly travel down that road by getting over that entrance?

I began to stretch my neck to see if any construction was in progress back there, but there was nothing I could see that suggested there was. I looked down at the ditch and tried to figure out how difficult it might be to get across. There was a small amount of green water at the bottom, and the ditch was probably three feet wide at the top. I thought I would be taking a chance from the top, so I decided I would step down the side of it, hop over the stagnant water, and climb up the other side. I looked around for the least difficult route and decided that there was no simple path.

I moved the grass around with my foot until I felt comfortable enough to step into the wiry weeds. I managed to make it the two feet or so down the side of the ditch without incident. I then began to examine the other side. It didn't seem like it was that far to jump from where I was standing, but my calculations suggested that one bad move might leave me sitting in a puddle of stagnant green water and I wouldn't be smelling of roses afterwards.

I heaved in a deep breath and leapt from my position on the side of the ditch. My foot caught the other side and then began to slide off of the red wet clay it had landed on, pulling my other foot down before it could land safely on the other side. I threw my body forward trying to break the slide, and I landed face first into a patch of prickly weeds. My face and arms screamed at me as my sneakers filled with green murky water from the bottom of the ditch. All of a sudden my beautiful walk had turned into an adventure.

I crawled up the side of the ditch to a clearing only a foot or two away. I tried to catch my breath, and then I began to assess the damage. The knees of my jeans were caked in rich red muddy clay, the bottoms around the ankles had turned a darker shade of blue from the water, and my sneakers bore strips of slimy green algae. My hands and arms were bleeding from thin long scratches, and I could only hope that my face was in better shape. All in all, I had suffered no major injuries. I stood up and placed a hand over my forehead to shield my eyes from the sun. I looked down the intriguing dirt road that had changed my course on this beautiful sunny afternoon and wondered where it would lead me.

The sky was so clear up ahead, and the few clouds that were in the sky looked like soft fluffy cotton balls. The woods seemed to narrow a bit as I took each step forward. It was odd to me how the woods looked as though they were clearer. The usual twigs and briars that grow amongst trees and bushes were not there. There were just beautiful trees and shrubs that seemed to have grown perfectly in size and shape. Then I saw a small gray rabbit pop out from a perfectly pruned tree stump, and it ran in front of me down the road that had brought me here in the first place. It seemed he was running ahead of me to warn someone or something that I was coming.

I watched the small gray creature hop ahead of me until it had dropped into a hole or perhaps thumped down a hill. And then I marveled at the beautiful scene that stretched out before me. There were clusters of foothills surrounding white-capped mountains, and right in the center I saw the most magnificent crystal blue mountain I had ever seen. The unusual road along which my feet were guiding me seemed to lead right through each foothill and mountain straight up to the blue gem of a sky. I was captivated by the way the dirt on the road looked as if it had turned golden from where I was standing.

I suddenly realized that there were a tremendous number of birds chirping all around me. It sounded like hundreds of them, of various kinds yet all of them singing the same soft melody. The breeze became even more pleasant than before, and although the sun was bright there was little heat beaming from it. The temperature, the weather, the view were all so perfect!

I kept my feet on the path of the trimmed dirt road, to become more beautiful with each step I took. I could see just a few yards in front of me a small rippling stream not much wider than the trench I had to cross only moments before. The fresh gurgling of water made me yearn to drink and to wash the dried blood and stagnant water that had dried on my body. My feet began to quicken, and my mouth became so dry that I could not get to the stream fast enough. The sounds of the rippling water and the birds melodically chirping made me wonder if I hadn't died when I slipped into that puddle of green water. The stream's water was so fresh—so cool on my lips, and I could feel it moving down my throat and through my veins with each swallow I took. I felt refreshed and renewed as if a new birth had taken place within me.

I rubbed me face and upper limbs with the cool water, and I instantly felt the same revival, only it was on the outside this time. The water soothed the screams of my wounds that had already started settling down, and it made me yearn to dip my sore aching feet into its clear pool of refreshing liquid. Then I felt my feet tingle as I plopped them gently into the stream's inviting waters.

I was soaking up all the pleasure this stream of living water could offer me when I heard the crisp crackling of dry leaves. I sat as still as possible to try and figure out which direction the noise was coming from. An old man popped out of a wooded area on the other side of the stream.

"Have you seen Miss Emily?" he asked. "One of her children has arrived. Have you seen her pass this way? I think she might have been with Mary Belle."

The old man who wore a gray beard extending down to his waist was wrenching his hands and pacing back and forth as though he were extremely upset.

"I haven't seen anyone…"

"I have to find Emily," he interrupted, and then he turned around and went back to the wooded area he had come from. It was as though he had never seen me and was merely asking himself the question.

I laughed out loud at what I had just seen. My voice echoed back with the melody of heavenly birds as I did so. I looked around the beautiful land that I had discovered and wondered if I wouldn't see the Mad Hatter rise up from out of a hole in the ground. This was so comical, and yet it was so real. I stared at the spot where the old man had entered, and I wondered if I should dare attempt another adventure today. The stream's water was now cold on my feet, and the large gray stone I had seated myself on was now telling my rear end that my sitting time was up. I picked up my sneakers and stuffed my socks inside them. Then clasping them between my fingers, I headed across the stream.

The sun glistened behind the trees, and I began thinking that getting off the main road had not been such a good idea. But I had become totally engrossed in this whole event that was unfolding before me, and knew that I must continue. If the old man, a lady named Emily and a lady named Mary Belle were lurking around in those woods, there certainly should have been no reason that I couldn't walk there either. I looked once again at the magical mountains before me. I took a deep breath and turned into the woods, wondering what kind of place it was in which I had found myself.

There was nothing rare or unique. For instance there was nothing prickly growing about the woods other than it was more serene than most. "Never, Never Land," I said out loud as I walked through this radiant natural forest. I was afraid of getting lost and I was about to turn around and head back when I saw another old man come from the woods in front of me. Something of a spectacle, he wore an old wool jacket and combat boots that had seen better days. His face was unshaven, and although he appeared old there were few wrinkles on his face. He wore a serious expression, and I felt as though I was about to be scolded.

"Who has brought you here? There is no record of your entrance," he blurted out, obviously in no need of an introduction.

"I…I saw an opening from the road and decided to hop the ditch to get across. I didn't know I needed to check in or anything. I…"

"Aha! I see. You need a lesson in Believe." Once more that day I had been interrupted. What was it about the people here? But his statement about a lesson in **Believe** had confused me, and I was more interested in knowing more about that.

"I need a lesson in what?"

The old man was smiling when he spoke. "Your faith must not be too strong, but your heart must be in the right place or you would have never made it to Believe. You are one of the lucky ones, you know? That window you came through is not opened to many. Although the Almighty One provides everyone with some sort of window, seldom does He use one quite this obvious." His smile displayed a stained set of teeth that weren't all accounted for.

"Let me get this straight. You are telling me that I have walked through a window into a different realm and am no longer in my world? Am I supposed to believe that? Who are you? Is this that Candid Camera Show? Where's the camera?" My grin was big, and I could feel laughter building up in my throat—the kind of laughter you experience as a child where all the emphasis is ejected from the inside out through loud contagious laughter. You know what I'm talking about: that big hearty laugh that feels good all over. Here I was standing in a flawless forest with a man who was wearing a wool jacket in ninety-degree weather and telling me that I am no longer in my world. Yeah, right.

He began to walk past me in the direction from which I had entered this forest. My feet followed him. They needed no directions, seeming as though they were on a mission all their own. He walked until he reached the side of the road where he stopped abruptly. I wasn't prepared for his pit stop, and I found myself preparing for a collision right into his back. At least I thought I would, but when I closed my eyes for the impact, I merely stopped and impacted on nothing. When I opened my eyes again, I saw that he was standing a foot away from me. At that moment I began to feel dizzy, as though my experience was a little too much for me. Perhaps this had been a bad idea. Then the old man raised his right hand and pointed up towards the mountain.

"This path was paved with love and kindness. Each golden brick that you see laid represents someone who has crossed over this window and experienced life to the fullest thereafter. The opportunity for you to see believe is the opportunity for you to live again with new life. There are no tricks or gimmicks. The decision to believe is one that only you can make."

The path glistened with golden rays. Bricks of gold now replaced the soil that had once been sand. The golden path led over every foothill and mountain, directly to the great majestic blue mountain that now visibly displayed three crosses—the middle one much larger than the other two. I gasped in awe to think that I might be near the hill or even walking on the same ground that He traveled upon. I suddenly felt the urge to run. I knew that He couldn't see me. I was a disappointment to Him, and I knew it. I kept saying I was going to get straight one day, but I hadn't, and here I was. WOW! Suddenly my salvation was a little more important to me than it had been. My husband, Jim, had been pushing me but I just thought there was no rush. Oh, why hadn't I listened to him?

I leaned over near the old man's ear, and I whispered to him. "Is He over there?" And I pointed up at the majestic blue thing in the sky.

"You foolish woman! He is everywhere! Do you think that He can see you only when you want Him to? He is omnipotent, don't you know that?" the old man asked as if I had disappointed him greatly.

I suddenly felt a flash of heat rush through my body. I think I knew at that moment what an ostrich must feel like just before it sticks its head in the ground.

"I know that He is everywhere, but I'm afraid to look up at Him or to talk with Him. I am not who He would have me be. I am not worthy to walk through your window. I should not be here at all," I said through uncontrollable sobs. My heart was aching, and I was praying that He would not show His wrath on me that day.

The old man turned his head sideways and spoke in a calm soothing voice, "He loves you anyway. He only asks that you believe and that you profess His love for you.

"I DO BELIEVE! I do know that He loves me, and I have always known," I screamed with sadness and relief. Then this indescribable joy swept over me. I cupped my hands over my face and wept. I cried until my soul was empty of all the pain and guilt that had ever dwelt within me. I cried until I was ready to go home and tell Jim that I was ready now. I was ready for the day when He would call my name.

When I brought my hands down from my face, I was standing on my own dirt lane and staring at my little farmhouse. My husband was sitting there patiently on the front porch swing. The porch light cast a glow on him that had made me think of an angel. My deep love for him rose to the surface, and I realized how much God loved me. God had sent this angel to me. He had been watching over me even when I was denying Him. Yes, God did love me, and He wanted me to know it before it was too late.

You might think that the sun got too hot for me that afternoon, or you might just down right not believe me, and that's okay. I believe that there is a place where love and kindness exists, and I only hope that it doesn't take a fall in a wide ditch with stagnant water to get you to believe. As for me, I plan on seeing that world again someday. Next time, I hope Jim will be with me.

JOHN 3:16: For God so loved the world that He gave His only begotten Son, that whosoever believeth in Him shall not perish, but have everlasting life.

Messages from Caroline

*T*hat old sign has stood on the side of the highway for just about as long as I can remember. You know the kind I'm talking about. It has those letters that you can change from time to time to put up different messages. Yep, that old sign has stood there since the church was built. And Preacher Tim has done a terrific job through the years, sending messages to the world and to the lost souls he hopes to someday save. I have been passing that old sign just about everyday throughout my adult life, and I have always enjoyed the Bible verses posted there, but it wasn't until Caroline came that I saw what glorious work the Lord intended to do with it.

The girl who first visited our church with rain dripping from her hair looked rather weak around the eyes, but otherwise she was a beautiful, dark-haired young woman who just appeared in our church one Sunday. She had a solemn way about her, and she never talked much about anything, yet her smile was contagious whenever she chose to display it. She eventually let her true heart show through that old sign out front. It took us some time to realize how important the sign was to her, but the work she did through it will never be forgotten by our little old church and the tiny hearts it reached. I'm not one to go around telling stories like this, but I have never seen anything like what she did in all my years, and I doubt that I ever will again.

She came one stormy morning right at the break at the beginning of fall. I remember when she walked in with her hair all slicked around her face from the rain that was coming down in torrents. She didn't seem bothered by the way the weather had drenched her hair, and she walked straight to the front pew and made herself comfortable. Our church was small, and we didn't see many guests dropping in often, so she was *noticed*. It seems that as times change, people prefer the big church to the smaller one. I for one preferred our little church that sits on the main highway running through Millsboro, and I particularly like the people. Preacher Tim always has a powerful sermon, and I always leave feeling renewed with the Spirit and love of God. Small was just fine with me and the rest of us, but then Caroline came and things started to happen—things that we all agreed must have been only that which was sent only by God.

We were all pretty shocked a few weeks later when the preacher suggested that she take over the messages on the sign. He had said he was tired and would love for her to help, and she had quickly and proudly accepted his offer. I'm not quite sure, but I think that was about the time that the dark lines under Caroline's eyes began to slowly fade. The very first message from Caroline read I AM ALWAYS WITH YOU EVEN UNTIL THE END, placed neatly on the sign that stood in front of our blessed little church.

That was quite soothing, I had thought as I passed it on my way to work. *Isn't it nice to know that He is always with us?* I whistled to myself as I traveled down Route 13 at its busiest hour of the morning trying to get to work on time. Even while I was at work that day, the sign lingered in my thoughts. What a powerfully short phrase for her to place on that little board. I suspected then that there was something about Caroline—something, that would eventually touch the hearts of us all. It wasn't merely just a sign anymore. I sensed that it was a note to someone or to everyone. I wasn't quite sure which.

Several days later I saw her standing beside the sign and waving at a school bus as it traveled past. There was such a glow in her eyes that I could even see it from where I sat in my car. She was wearing a smile that caused me to smile at nothing. It felt good to see her smile like that. The solemn girl who had walked into church that cold, wet morning was slipping away; and if God could light up someone like Caroline whose dark rings no longer existed, then surely He had more gifts in store for her. If only we had known. Perhaps things could have been different had we only known what Caroline was doing there.

And so it went that each Monday morning as I traveled down Highway 13 to go to work, I would pass Caroline out in front of her sign. There would be a new message, and she would be smiling and waving at the bus that drove past. I often wondered if it was the same bus or all of the buses. Whatever the case was, her huge smile must have radiated in every direction. I looked forward in the early morning hours to passing Caroline with that wide smile on her face, waving franticly at a bus filled with children.

One Wednesday, right after evening services, Caroline stood up and asked the congregation to pray for her. White streaks ran down her soft pink cheeks, and the grief expressed on her brow was painful just to look at. She did not comment on her request, and no one felt as though it were his or her business to ask. I did notice, however, that not one member of our small congregation walked past Caroline that evening without giving her a hug or a handshake. She had made her way into our family of God quite quickly, and she gained our love just as fast. Even I walked over to Caroline and told her that she would *always* be in my prayers. Just in the short time I had known her, she had become a blessing to me each morning, and I looked forward to seeing her smiling face by the road. She gently grabbed my hand and said, "I have finally found my home here. God bless you people for allowing me to be a part of it." Then she walked off into the ladies' room, obviously holding back sobs she wasn't ready to share with the world.

Caroline kept placing her precious messages out front come rain or shine, and our little church watched as one visitor after another stopped in to hear the Word of God. Preacher Tim said that most of his visits with our guests had revealed that they were touched by the sweet innocent words placed on our sign out front by Caroline. Her tender thoughts were reaching the world in the most loving way.

One morning a few months after Caroline started doing our sign, I saw her outside by the sign blowing kisses at the bus that passed our little church. Right behind her on the sign were the words, GOD WATCHES OVER HIS CHILDREN AND PROTECTS THEM. Again, I couldn't help but wonder about her fascination with the children on that bus. She was determined to make sure they saw her as well as the messages she placed on that sign.

Spring began to settle in around Millsboro, and the branches were budding into beautiful green leaves. The ground was covered in fresh colored flowers, and the membership of our church had doubled. All sorts of new people were making their way into our church, and the men had to open the upper part of the sanctuary again—a part that hadn't been used in many years. There was laughter and fellowship like nothing I had seen in all my years there. The Spirit of God was emanating throughout our little church, and a lot of the credit went to Caroline and the wonderful way God was using her. Our little congregation of worshippers was being blessed by her presence in so many ways.

One evening Preacher Tim started off his service by thanking Caroline and asking her to speak on behalf of her work on the old sign out front. He told the congregation that she had something she would like to say. Caroline rose from her seat and walked to the altar where the preacher stood. At that moment I noticed how small she had become. The dark rings were gone from under her eyes, and her face glowed from the Spirit. But even though the dark rings were gone, they were replaced by a sunken look, and her body did not look healthy at all. Her tiny frame of hanging flesh suggested to me that she was losing weight much too quickly. Caroline looked as though she were just dwindling away.

She stood behind the podium and thanked the preacher for his kindness, and then a solemn look swept over her as she began a short speech that I vaguely remember now, except for the end. Caroline had everyone's attention when she closed the end of her brief talk about the messages on the sign. This is what I remember her saying, word for word:

"Some of you have seen me out front waving at the school bus as it passes by each morning, and I'm sure some of you have even wondered what it is that I'm doing out there so early in the morning. Well, I want you to know that that little school bus holds something very dear to me: my children. You see, I haven't seen them in five years, except for in the morning as they pass to go to school."

She paused as though one more word might cause the stream of tears she was holding back to start spilling over in buckets. Then she proceeded, "You see, I didn't always live my life right, and I lost them to my mother. She raises my children for me and does a good job, but she won't let me see them. She thinks that I'm not worthy of their love, and she is probably right. Even so, there are so many things that I wish to tell them, and with the help of Preacher Tim and God, I have been able to do so.

"Several months ago, I discovered that my heart is very weak and I need a new one in order to carry on in this world. Well, the time is drawing near, and I guess God has other things in store for me. Whatever the case may be, I know He gave me the chance to share my love and thoughts with my children, and for this I am truly thankful."

Her eye glistened with tears that struggled to break through the dam she had built in front of them, and as her voice cracked she said, "Keep me in your prayers. God bless you all for being so wonderful to me."

She hobbled away from the podium in complete silence. Limping back to her seat on the front pew and wiping the tears from her eyes as she opened her hymnbook, she led the congregation in singing,

"Amazing Grace." The room filled with the sweetest music I have ever heard coming from within the walls of the sacred building we worshipped in, and it was so pure that night as though perhaps there was a much bigger choir singing with us and joining in our praises to God. I wouldn't have been surprised to see a thousand angels hovering over us that night.

It wasn't long before we all noticed how weak Caroline was becoming. Bart Fields, the choir director, offered to take over the messages for her, but she wouldn't hear of it. That was her sign and her messages, and by the grace of God she planned on waving to her children everyday that she had left on this earth. Even Preacher Tim had been by to visit with Caroline's mother to let her know how sick she was, but Edith Snow would not even come to the door to let him in. Our whole church watched with sadness as Caroline drew nearer her last days without spending a moment with the three children she loved so dearly. Prayer chains were made to help call on God for this sad event that was taking place, and still Caroline's mother would have nothing to do with our church or the people in it.

As the season once again changed and the holidays arrived, we all noticed that the dark lines had reappeared on Caroline's face. There was not much sparkle left, and we knew that we had to do something for Caroline before it was too late. Sadie Thomas passed around a little flyer to the ladies of our church for an emergency meeting on behalf of poor Caroline. As each lady received her invitation, she accepted it with a discreet nod.

We stayed after the service that night, and Sadie got right to the point. "We're meeting here this evening because Caroline is getting worse, and it doesn't look as though the heart she has been waiting for is going to be found. I have gone out of my way, ladies, to try and make something happen here.

"As most of you know, my cousin Sarina is the vice-principal at the middle school, and she has agreed to let us discreetly take the kids by for a visit to see their mother. This has to be done in the strictest of confidence, and we must never let their grandmother know about it. Sarina would lose her job, and the rest of us would probably face legal charges. I know this is not the way we normally do things, but I've been praying about this and I believe God will not look upon me too harshly for this act of disobedience. I guess the next thing I need to do is get support from the rest of you ladies. I'm making a motion. Do I hear a second?"

Seconds came from all around the room. Not a person there was thinking about the consequences of what we were about to do. Caroline would see her children one more time before she found her heavenly home (the Lord willing). We carefully made plans for how we were going to get the children and where we would take them. The room was humming, and the excitement brought forth an aura in that room that I had never seen before that night. We packed up our notes and headed out the door giving hugs and good wishes for our venture. We all had a part to play in this deed, and everyone was pleased to be included.

The next morning the preacher phoned to let me know that Caroline had gotten real sick during the night and had been taken to the hospital. He asked me to get the prayer chain started at our church because it wasn't looking good for her here on this earth. I began calling without hesitation.

"Lord, be with Caroline through this most difficult time. We ask that Thy will and not our will be done. We also plead with You, dear Father, that Caroline get the opportunity to say farewell to her children. Amen."

My first phone call was to Sadie Thomas, and she phoned her cousin Sarina as soon as we ended our conversation. The time had come for Caroline to visit one last time with her children.

The plan was put into action before ten o'clock that morning. My job was to bring the children to the local hospital where Caroline was lying weakly among the sick. I picked up the children, explaining to them that their mother was very ill and I thought it would be nice for them to see her.

Their little eyes lit up with an excitement I could not understand but could see so well. I felt good about this. Hopefully God was pleased with this act of love our church wanted so much to do for Caroline. Surely God was pleased. I was blessed, and these children were loved—not just by their mother, but also by the entire church, although most had never met them. Somehow these children, despite who they were or how we met them, had become our children.

Sadie was waiting in the brightly colored sitting area at the entrance of the hospital when we walked through the sliding glass doors with the children. She bent down in front of them, introduced herself, and asked them their names. There was Eden, the youngest of the three, with her mother's dark hair and a bright smile that emitted the excitement of seeing her mother somewhere besides along the highway waving at them. Standing beside her was Jacob who was the oldest, carrying around a whole lot of hurt behind those beautiful dark eyes that mixed beautifully with his olive complexion. Next to Jacob and standing tall, there was Rebecca. Her fair complexion and blue eyes looked so different from her siblings. I assumed that she had inherited some of these features from her father. She was much more assertive than the other two. It was almost as though Rebecca knew why she was there. She seemed unafraid but hurried, as though she had to get inside the room where her mother was lying before it was too late. You could tell she didn't want to waste time on introductions because she kept asking, "Which way is she?"

Sadie cut the introductions short, and they headed down the hall. I sat down in one of the orange chairs that filled the waiting room, and picked up a magazine. I could not focus on the articles. I could only think of Caroline who had until two-thirty with her children, and I had no problem waiting for them. *"Lord, please let this be a blessing both to the children and to Caroline. Amen."*

It was nearing our time to leave when I saw the children walking down the long corridor. Their eyes were swollen, and their little cheeks were rosy red. I pondered what I might say to them as they drew nearer. I settled for silence. It seemed to be what the children needed most—and time to think about their visit with their sick mother.

We walked silently to the car, and the ride back to school was without words. It wasn't an uncomfortable silence, although it was quite solemn. Something in the way they all relaxed in my car assured me they were a little more at peace than they had been when I had picked them up that morning. Their empty eyes were now filled with a peace I had not seen before, yet their pain could not be hidden either.

I pulled up to the school and opened the car door. Each child got out mechanically and started walking towards the entrance. I bid them goodbye, and they headed towards the front entrance where buses were now pulling up and waiting for the bell to ring, sending forth a mob of excited children ready to return home. Watching as they walked towards the school, I saw Eden stop in her tracks and come running back to me. Her eyes were anxious and her arms were outstretched as she landed in my arms.

"Thank you for taking me to see Mom before she goes to heaven," she said as the tears rolled down her soft pink cheeks. "Mom says that God wants her up in heaven to do some work for Him there. Could you ask Him for me to let her stay down here a little while longer? I just haven't seen her in a long time, and I'd hate for her to go so soon. Will you *pleeease* do that for me?"

"Of course I will, honey." I said as I swallowed a large lump of heartache in my throat. "I don't know that He'll listen though."

"Well, just ask Him that Thy will be done and not my will, okay? That's what Mom told me I should ask. Will you do that for me?"

"Of course I will, dear. But you know that you can talk to Him too, whenever you want. Just close your eyes and put your hands together like this." I placed her tiny hands together in a praying position. "And you can tell Him whatever you need to, okay?"

"Okay." She turned to walk back to her siblings and stalled for just a moment. Turning around, she hugged my neck. "Thank you," she said with tears welling up in her eyes again. Then I watched as she walked back to her siblings who were waiting patiently for her and fighting back their own tears.

The drive back home seemed much longer than usual that day. The lump in my throat kept coming back with the slightest thought of those children. I felt exhausted, and I couldn't wait to take a nice hot bath to cleanse away some of the heavy burdens that had somehow made their way onto my shoulders. A hot bath and a long prayer was my vision as I drove back home.

The phone was ringing when I walked through my front door, and I stumped my toe on the corner stand next to the phone trying to get it before the person on the other end hung up. "Hello," I answered through that agonizing pain we have all felt after a good stump of a toe. "Yes…Yes…Yes…Okay." I hung up the phone. *Thank God we had gotten the children today. Tomorrow would have been too late.* I slid down the foyer wall and wept for what seemed like hours. The pain in my toe was suddenly forgotten.

I floated through the next few days, not being able to erase the little eyes filled with excitement that I had seen only a couple of days ago, and thinking that they were now filled with such grief. The funeral was packed with church members and others who had fallen in love with Caroline in front of her little sign out front. But it was after the funeral that God showed His amazing grace.

Edith Snow had brought the children to say goodbye to their mother, and she seemed to be grieving herself. She made her way over to me as people began to leave the church's sad gathering, and she introduced herself. She struggled to continue, and then she told me that the children had told her what we had done. And she would forever be grateful that the children had seen their mother before she passed away.

Well, Edith Snow is now seen each Sunday morning with the children, and Rebecca has even taken over the messages on the sign that her mother had expressed so much love from. Edith has graciously accepted God and has led her wonderful grandchildren to Him as well. Caroline still lives inside each of those tiny beautiful faces that we have come to look forward to seeing each week, and the congregation has adopted these children as our own.

Oh, and about the sign. When we left the cemetery the day of Caroline's funeral, we noticed that the sign out front of the church had been changed. The words, "WEEP NOT; SHE IS NOT DEAD, BUT SLEEPETH" were displayed neatly on the sign. We have never known who put that message out front, but some say it was God, letting His little children know that all was well with their mother who now resides in heaven, watching over her children from a beautiful star up above until she can reunite with them once again.

The Man I Am

No, I am not insane. I saw what I say I saw, and that is final! I came from a family with no background in mental illness, and I suffered very little as a child. I know what I am talking about. There is no logical explanation for it, therefore it must be God. You see, I am unworthy of even telling you that I know Him because I fail Him more times than I wish to admit. Yet He was there. He was present, and I have never experienced anything more fulfilling in my life. It was so long ago, and yet it seems like only days have passed since the whole thing took place. I was standing right there, and it happened before my very eyes. To this day people think I have lost my mind.

The line at the Men's Auxiliary food bank was quite long that day, and I had been standing there for quite some time. I had been on a three-day binge, and my head was kind of bothering me. But after seeing the children and their little hungry faces, I knew I had to come out from under Satan's curse and take care of my family. That's what I was doing in the food bank line.

My wife, Sarah Leigh, was a good woman. She put up with too much, if you ask me, but she was a fine woman just the same. I hadn't made life easy for her and our five children, but she never took to calling me names or putting me down. She had worked as a housemaid for the local doctor in town and only received a small pittance of a salary, and that's how we survived—except maybe when I could make it home from an odd job without hitting Harry's Harbor and spending it all out on liquor.

It was real hot that day, and I thought for sure the sweat was going to drain from my body enough so that I would shrivel up like a raisin. I was thinking about plopping myself down on the ground and perhaps scooting my way up the line when I saw it, him, or whatever. It moved so quickly behind the building that I wasn't sure if the sun was just playing tricks on my mind. Yet I knew it, and I felt it. I had the sudden urge to jump from my place in the line that was now creeping up to about the halfway point, but something held me back from doing it. Logic. Logic was telling me that nothing had *whooshed* around that corner and that I should lay off the cheap liquor and perhaps find a way to buy the more expensive stuff. But then, I saw it again. It was just as quick, but I knew that it was *something* this time. Curiosity filled my soul, and I reluctantly stepped from my precious spot in line. I felt foolish for leaving the line that I had been standing in for hours taking up my whole day, and yet the thing was drawing me towards it where it would be waiting.

I turned the corner of the white cinder block building that was covered in flakes of black mildew, and it seemed as though the sun went down. I could feel goose bumps rising on my arms from the chill that had surrounded me. It couldn't be possible that the air could turn so cold so quickly. I tried to pace my breath as I strolled towards an old Dempsey Dumpster that had a wooden bushel basket sitting next to it. The flies were swarming all around it—there must have been hundreds of them. I drew nearer to the basket and feared looking into it, afraid of what I might discover sitting in the bottom of it. The stench of something strong filled the air as I moved towards it.

The dead fish and bones that lay at the bottom of the old bushel basket reeked of a stench I cannot describe to you, but I was relieved that it was only dead fish. Then from behind the dark green dumpster there appeared something as if from an old horror spoof. I heard a noise. It sounded like the static you might hear on a television with bad reception. My feet led me around the old rusting rack of iron, yet there was hesitation within me. I can't describe it; I can only say that I sensed there was something *not right*. The static became clearer, and I realized that the sounds I was hearing were those of even more flies. They were in swarms and were diving towards the ground, then returning back up towards my waistline, and they had teeth! Not great big fangs, but tiny miniscule needle like teeth. They were carrying what appeared to be something of a fleshy substance. It was then that I knew I must bend down and look through the swarm of flies that huddled around some flesh-like object lying on the ground.

The humming became louder, and they began landing on my face and arms. I swatted at them with both hands flailing in the air, but there seemed no fear in these mini beasts. I was about to draw back from the unbelievable attack that had begun taking place on me when I saw him. He was lying there, and his head was twisted in a rather uncompromising way. Thinking that he looked like someone I knew, I realized that it was my jacket he was wearing! That filthy no good thief had somehow managed to get my old wool jacket from me and had the nerve to turn around and break his neck in it!

I reached down to lift his head so I could get a better look at his face, fighting the torrent of razor-toothed flies as I did so. His hair was gray, and it looked as though he had never run a comb through it. I felt a kind of sympathy for this man who had died back here all alone behind the Men's Auxiliary, lying in the stench of decay and rubble. It was then that I saw his hand. The old bum was wearing my wedding band, too? I stared into the dead man's eyes, and I realized where I knew him from. He was me! How could that be? How could I be looking down at my own dead body?

Almost as if to answer my question that I hadn't orally asked, it came forward and began to moan out sentences, "This is the life of Fred Grimes who chose to drink his family's profits away and cast them to the welfare of his town. He spent his earnings on drink and gambling. After one good night of gambling, he left the bar and was accosted by thieves more desperate than he. He fought a good fight but was powerless without the help of the Holy One."

"Nooo!" I screamed at the thing that looked like a cross between a human being and some sort of shadow. "I cannot be dead if I am standing here talking to you! How can you try and make me think that this is my body that lies here in filth?"

The wind began to blow a little, and the thing's clothing that draped over its frame swayed in the wind. "You have disappointed the One who has created you, and yet He knows your heart and wishes for you to turn from your damaging ways. You have children at home dependent upon your guidance. You must leave your evil ways."

"How dare you say I guide my children astray! Sarah Leigh strives daily to educate them and feed them. She works for them and pays our bills nicely." I sneered at this thing that I felt was compelled to send me to my knees begging to wake me from my nightmare.

"The Father has seen great defiance from you, and you will be required to stand before Him some day. What shall you say to him, *'Why Father, my wife was the head of my home and my family, and I needn't have done a thing for them'*? Will that be the excuse you'll make to the Father of all fathers?"

I began to despise the thing that stood before me, and I wanted more than anything to curse him until he cowered away. But with my uncertainty as to how I would be left at his departure (standing or lying in filth, dead), I chose not to.

Hadn't it been the truth, though? I was merely a worthless old drunk who let his wife take care of him. Not much of a man, huh? "I have much to offer my family!" I screamed back at him. I was the smartest kid in my class! I went on science trips that only those described as geniuses could attend. Don't tell me that I have nothing to offer my family! The fierceness of my dislike for this *thing* was becoming all the more obvious.

"You speak the truth. However, you offer your family nothing, and that is what our Father sees. He knows your heart and believes that you are blind to what you are doing. Your last opportunity to accept Him and to let Him in is knocking at your door today. How will you answer the One who is the greatest of all?"

My knees began to quiver, and I found myself kneeling on the gravel and mud surrounding the trash bin. I suddenly felt so small. Certainly I had not seen myself in such a light as this before. Had I been so shallow as to neglect my own flesh and blood, my own children? Could it be that this creature that stood before me knew more about what kind of man I am than I did myself? Certainly our Father knows that I am a good man and have never done anyone harm. He must see that I walk this life without trampling a soul, except perhaps my poor Sarah Leigh. Surely, our Father must see that."

There seemed to be a pause as though this thing was thinking of his response, and then before my eyes he began to lift up towards the sky the lower portion of his body, stretching in a trail behind him. "You must go now and heed the word of Our Father. Stop pondering the past, and look forward to your restoration." The wind whistled as the figure that had communicated with me lifted up into the heavens, and I began to weep.

The flies were swarming all around me when I felt someone kick my side and ask, "Hey mister, are you going to lay there or are you planning on moving up the line?" *Had I been dreaming? Was all that I had experienced been but a figment of my imagination?* I rubbed my brow and looked at the older fellow behind me who looked like he could use a good meal. He sure didn't seem to have much to smile about.

I looked over at the side of the old concrete building and wondered what I might find back there. The compulsion became too great, and I stepped out of the food line for what seemed like the second time that day. I walked around the side of the building, expecting the cold air to again sweep over me as it had done before. But just a cool dampness was in the air from the building blocking the sun's rays. I looked ahead and saw the bushel basket just as I had seen it before beside the old Dempsey Dumpster. Only this time there was something hovering inside of it. My feet carried me straight to it without my moving a muscle. There was no sound of the buzzing that had filled the air earlier, and no sign of any flies anywhere.

As I peered inside the basket, I found enough bread and meat to feed my family for a week, and at the very bottom there was a fine men's suit just my size.

I can tell you that I picked that bushel basket up and took it home. I used the suit to go out and find a job, and I worked to become the man I am. I worked in the engineering department of a horticulture plant until I retired seven years ago.

Sarah Leigh passed on four years ago, but not without seeing her Fred become the man she had envisioned him to be. I took my children to church and taught them the true meaning of love. They suffered greatly in their younger years, and this I can never make up to them. However, I can love them the rest of my life and make them glad to have known me. For I'm the one who introduced them to the greatest one of all—our heavenly Father.

So you laugh at me and tell me that I am insane, and perhaps I will even laugh with you. But I know what I saw that day, and I shall never forget the unrelenting debt I owe to the One who loves me so much. The man I am today is the man my God intended me to be.

I John 3:8: *He that committeth sin is of the devil; for the devil sinneth from the beginning. For this purpose the Son of God was manifested, that He might destroy the works of the devil.*

Renewing Hope

She held her breath as she entered the room. Everyone was sitting so straight on the old wooden pews that lined the church. Up ahead was the mahogany altar that she had become so accustomed to seeing each Sunday morning. Making her way up to the front, she looked to see if perhaps this morning that dreaded pew would be taken and she could hide somewhere in the back. Ever since *it* happened, her mother had made her sit there. Mom had insisted that she would find comfort in God's Word. It did seem to help, at least while she was here. To her dismay, she found the pew empty—almost as though it had been waiting for her, even welcoming her to rest her weary soul.

Last night had been a long one. The dreams seemed to be more real now than they had been before. She spent her nights running from him in her dreams, constantly looking over her shoulder as if to find him there smiling that hellish grin that assured her there was no remorse in his heart. His twisted eye glared off into some unknown realm that made her think of what hell might be like. She hated sleeping now, if she could call it sleep. There seemed to be no peace at anytime of the day, but the nights were the most terrifying. Even here at church, she had thought she heard his voice once. It had turned out to be the guest speaker for that night, but somehow *he* still had managed to follow her. Even though most of it was in her mind he was still there, taunting her and making life miserable. She would never forget that night.

The organ began to fill the room with a joyful invitation that she used to look forward to hearing on Sunday morning. But this morning she seated herself on the gold velvet cushion that was so worn from use, and she sulked. She wondered when the preacher might reupholster the seats. If you asked her, it was about time to fix them. Then the music director came to the podium and directed the congregation to stand. All rose with a hymnbook in hand.

The dark-haired man with a bushy mustache cleared his throat as he asked every one to turn to page 246. Charity could clearly see that the man was nervous. He had only done this twice before here at church, and his insecurities were obvious by the twisting of his hands. The preacher had been delighted when he finally found someone who could take over the choir. He was getting up there in years now, and he was ready for a rest. Mr. Thomas was the most fitting for this position. He had an excellent singing voice, and his demeanor was so serene. The sound of the congregation brought her back to the room. They were singing "When the Roll is called Up Yonder."

She wondered if *he* would be there when the roll was called up yonder. She wondered if God would forgive him for the things *he* had done to her. It somehow didn't seem fair to her that God would let someone like that get through the gates of heaven. Charity decided right then and there that she didn't want to go to heaven if he was going to be there. Then she thought of her options. Well, maybe she did want to go to heaven anyway.

"Good morning," a voice called to her as she drifted back to the church and away from her intense thoughts of the hereafter. The congregational greeting was in full swing. She wondered how many songs they had sung and how much she had missed while she was lost in her thoughts. This was her favorite part of the morning. The members of the church were always so kind and caring. She liked knowing that they cared about her, and she prayed for them every night.

After everyone was seated again, the preacher asked them to turn to Hosea 14:9. Then he went on to talk about the Lord and said that *His ways were right*. "The just," he said, "would walk in His ways, and the transgressors would fall." She listened intently as he talked of what this message meant. She heard him say that God has a way of allowing things to happen, but He doesn't cause them to happen. He talked of what happens to those who choose to disobey God, and how we are all responsible for our actions. She knew that was right. She could have said *no* to Heidi when she had asked her to come with them. Never mind that she had trusted Heidi. Mother still would not have approved, and Charity knew that. Heidi was supposed to have been her best life-long friend, not the traitor she winded up being. She heaved in her breath deeply and thought away Heidi and *the other two*. She wanted no memories that reminded her of that night. The preacher was right. We do have to pay for our wrong deeds, and Charity learned quickly that paying for wrong doings could sometimes be painful.

Mom had told her that she was lucky he hadn't done more to her, and she should be thankful that it didn't turn out to be a rape case. She knew Mom didn't say that to be hurtful, but because it was true. Charity knew that her mother was right, but it didn't help her feel any better. He had still frightened her so terribly. They didn't understand that it wasn't so much what he did that night that hurt so much as what he had done to her faith in her fellow man. She had never been as frightened in all her life as she was that terrible night out with Heidi.

The preacher's voice broke through her thoughts, and this time coming back had caused her to jump a little off her seat. She looked around to see if anyone had noticed. Her soft pink cheeks seemed to deepen even more when she saw that the guest singer for the morning was looking at her and smiling. She had seen it all, and Charity could see that on her face. The lady's eyes were soft and warm, and Charity felt warm all over when she looked into them.

The sermon was soon over, and Charity could feel her heart becoming a little less angry with him. Mom was right about coming here. She could feel some relief in her heart, and even her shoulders were loosening some. She knew the preacher knew what he was talking about. God takes care of every wrongdoing, and he would take care of this too. She knew this in her heart; she just had to keep remembering it in her head. Everything would turn out all right. It always did. Thank the Lord.

The preacher turned to introduce the pretty woman who had seen Charity jump out of her seat earlier. Her name was Bonnie Fields, and she sounded as beautiful as she looked to Charity. The woman looked young, although the gray in her hair suggested that she was older. The words that came from her lips were so soft and kind. Charity listened as Ms. Fields sang old hymns that Grandma had sung to her on the old front porch swing to put her to sleep when she was little. The tears rolled down her cheeks as she thought of Grandma. She had always called Charity by her middle name, Hope, and she had said it in a way that made it sound almost comical. *"Good things come to those who wait,"* Grandma had always said. Charity didn't know what that meant before, but she felt that she was beginning to understand a whole lot more than she used to.

Ms. Field's words filled the room once again as she went on to describe her next song. She had written it for her mother because she had been hurt so many times by her husband, Ms. Fields' father. She said that she had watched her mother being abused since she was very small, and that she had still wound up being successful just by putting her faith in God. Charity's spine tingled as she thought that God could also make her pain and anguish go away if she would just give it to Him and believe He had something wonderful planned for her.

"I want you to know, kids," Ms. Fields had said as she looked straight into Charity's eyes, "circumstances don't have to control your destiny. God can take you any where."

Charity listened as the words of Ms. Fields' song filled the room. The tears poured down her cheeks as she thought of her older sister, Chastity, whose middle name was Faith. Their Mother had always said she would "always have Faith and Hope." The girls knew that she was referring to them, but they also knew that she was referring to her faith and hope in the Lord.

Charity thought of how, in spite of losing Daddy at an early age, Mom had always kept her faith and hope. Somehow she would make Christmas happen for the two girls even though the entire year would be filled with many great struggles. She always had a smile on her face in the darkest of times. She said that those were the times she was tested by the devil the most, and so in those times she leaned even more on the Lord.

Tingles went up and down Charity's spine as she thought of how she was her mother's Hope and she was therefore Hope. She would not be called Charity any more; she would be called by her middle name to constantly remind her that hope can bring you through so many difficult trials. In her mind's eye, she captured a light that shone so brilliantly upon her face, and she saw a hand reaching towards hers. It was the hand that would lead her and guide her through her darkest hour—the hand that had been there when the phone rang that night and awakened her only to find *him* standing over her grinning with the dirtiest look she had ever seen on a human being's face. It was the hand that had taken care of her, her Mom and Chastity throughout the years. God was good, and she knew it!

The preacher's invitation broke through her thoughts, but this time she returned calmly. His words were inviting those who wished to be saved and wanted to get to know God more personally to come forward and make the first step towards living life right. She had been baptized when she was twelve, and until today she had not known what getting to know God would be like. The altar appeared to be so far away. Her legs were pulling her up off the seat, and she was floating towards the front knowing that there was a meaning in her life and that hope was restored. She told the preacher that she was ready to give God everything because she knew that God had given her everything. They prayed together, and Charity cried even more. The tears were not tears of sadness but of joy—joy because *he* wasn't going to ruin another day in her life, and because she had forgiveness and even a little sympathy for his sad pathetic life. God is so good.

The ride back home was a quiet one. Her mother had very little to say except that she loved her and was so proud of her. Her mother was like that, always knowing when to just let things go quietly along. She never pushed her to talk about things that were troubling her; she would simply offer a reminder that she was there whenever the time was right for talking. Charity was lucky for that, and she knew it. That's why she thanked God every night for her mother, the best friend she had ever known.

When the car stopped in the driveway, Charity was pushing her way to the front door. There was something that she had to do, and she had to do it right away. Later would be too late. Up the stairs she went, taking two at a time. When she reached her room, she went straight to the corner and lifted the edge of the Oriental rug that matched her room so well. Mother had a wonderful way of coordinating things. Charity remembered the day Mom had put it down, and how she had thrown such a fuss over the design. Mom had said it would look great when she was finished, and she had been right. She lifted one of the boards in the hardwood floor below the carpet and pulled out an antique cigar box that had now been covered with material and lace. Mom had taught her how to do that when she was younger. She flipped open the lid and there it was.

She drew in a deep breath and then pulled the light blue ribbon she had been wearing that night out of the box. Her eyes filled with tears as she balled it tightly in her hand. "Please God, let this be the end of the nightmares, and let the memories of *him* forcing a kiss on me fade away. Give me the strength that I need to put this all behind me," she prayed.

She headed down the stairs with the ribbon still tightly clasped in her hand, and she headed straight for the garage where Mom kept her gardening tools. She looked around the cold dark room and finally found what she had been looking for. The small hand tools were all neatly placed in a drawer; Charity grabbed the small shovel that Mom used to plant new flowers and put bulbs in the ground. She then headed back outside and out back towards the woods. Way back there she would find a good place not so close to home, but not too far away, either. She might need to remind herself someday of the great things that had taken place inside her heart this very perfect fall day.

She followed the trail for a while, and then she got off of it near a fallen tree that had been one of last year's victims of a terrible ice storm. Then she fell to her knees and began to shovel right next to a hole that looked as if it belonged to a groundhog. There were lots of different kinds of animals that could have built their home in a thicket like that, but somehow Charity knew it was the home of a groundhog. When she finally had dug deep enough, she opened the hand that had been carrying the ribbon, and she dropped it inside the dark hole.

The words of her grandmother again came to her mind—words that had such little meaning to her until this morning—and she felt the burning desire to say them out loud.

"Hear me speedily, O Lord," she said through a weak and crackling voice. "My spirit faileth: hide not Thy face from me, lest I be like unto them that go down into the pit."

She knew her anger would take her down into a pit, and she knew that's why she had to rid herself of that anger. Into the hole went the horrid look of his face, the betrayal of her friend Heidi who had gotten amnesia when asked about the evening in question. And into the hole went all the misery that came with the entire ugly event that had occurred that dreadful night. And last but not least, into the hole went Charity—the little girl who had carried so many unnecessary burdens in her heart. Mom had been right when she had said she would always have Hope and Faith, and she would never again walk without Hope.

She placed her hands in the dark soil and began to cover the ribbon that she had worn that night. Then she packed it down tightly as she took two sticks and tied them together with a vine, making the rugged form of a cross. She placed it on the freshly disturbed earth. She stood up from her squatting position that was now beginning to make her legs ache, and she wiped the soil from her knees. Then smearing the tears that slid down her cheeks with the soil on her hands, Hope walked out of the woods freshly renewed and ready to live life to its fullest. Thanks to Grandma, Mom and mostly God, Hope was renewed and God was so good.

The Thicket

There are no miracles where I come from. People walk around in sad somber moods, blaming others for all the miserable things in their lives. They refused to try and change anything, much less themselves. They were trapped in a life of misery because they could not understand anything that was not of their norm. There *was* someone once who claimed to have experienced a miracle. I personally never wanted to believe him, but I know something about his miracle that I have never told anyone. I never told because there were no miracles in Essex County. The people there scoffed at those who claimed to have experienced miracles or anything that could be perceived as such a thing. So I watched my mouth when I was out there among them. Or at least I did up until last fall.

I saw something then that I can't explain away. I saw it all occur, and I still sometimes try and push it to the back of my mind because it is not logical. It makes no sense, and yet it does. I decided that day that I would have to face the sneers and ridicules of those who wanted nothing more than to belittle my story and me. I could not keep the tale within me. It was just too much. You may not believe it, but I'm telling you that I experienced something that was not of this earth.

I work at the old sawmill off Copper Road in Essex County, and I have a good mile and a half to walk home each day. That's never bothered me because I love the exercise, and there's nothing like taking a long walk on a beautiful day—in fact even on a not so beautiful day. I somehow can find all kinds of things to be grateful for as I look up at the sky and watch the wind move the tree limbs back and forth on a windy day. Even on the coldest days of the year, I can find some beauty that most men seem to neglect—like the icicle that dangles from a branch, or the snowflakes that fall, each one distinct from the other. Isn't it amazing how the tiniest things in life can bring out the best in us?

Well, I was walking home one evening, and it was right after the time had changed in the fall, so it was getting dark earlier. I was heading down the old dirt lane that leads away from the mill and was nearing the part where the woods become quite thick before one gets to the main road when I heard some noises coming from within a thicket. I couldn't help myself but to stop and listen to try and figure out what this noise was. Since I walked home regularly, I was familiar with most all of the sounds, and this one sounded like nothing I could identify. So naturally—to try and please my curiosity—I began to step slowly toward the noise that baffled me so.

It was kind of like a *click, click, click* and then a *jangle, jangle, jangle*. It wasn't getting louder, and it wasn't getting any softer. It was just a constant monotonous sound in the woods coming from the thicket. I tried to get my head in through some of the thick briars and thorns, hoping to see inside of this thicket that had aroused my curiosity. The thorns began almost immediately to prick my face, and I had to withdraw. I was not going to find out what was in the thicket that way.

I browsed around the edge of the woods to see if perhaps there was a ready-made trail close by. Nothing that I could see looked like an easy way of entering the not so inviting forest. But ahead of me I saw what looked like an opening. It was by no means an opening that would allow a human through it unscathed, but it was an opening. I walked towards it kicking up dust from the dry dirt lane that I trod each day. I peered into the opening and tried to figure out how difficult it might be to travel past the briars and branches that were hovering all around it. It didn't look easy, but it looked possible. Therefore, it *was* possible. I would attempt to make my way through in order to see what it was that I was hearing.

I stepped into the forest and felt the autumn sun disappear from my face. A slight chill filled the air. Then something came sweeping past my feet, and it caused me to jump and fall sideways on an old tree trunk that looked as though it had been there for many years. I felt a small trickle of blood drip from off my forehead and onto my nose. I had managed to fall right under the biggest thorn bush in the whole forest, or at least it looked that way to me. I pushed myself up to a sitting position with my right hand that was now aching from trying to catch my fall, and I looked around me. I could hear the sound better now, and I wasn't quite sure why. It seemed to me as though it was coming down from underneath me, but I knew that that could not be possible. So I pushed myself up on my knees and began to try and make a full stand. The little squirrel that had thrown me off my course was now hiding in a small hollow of a tree staring at me as if to see what move I'd make next.

"Sorry," I whispered to the little creature as I wiped the soil from the side of my trousers. I couldn't believe how bad I felt for frightening the little creature, but I truly felt sad that he had been frightened so.

Once back to my mission, I began reaching up to the sky and grabbing hold of branches so I could pull them back to pass through without scratching myself too much. It seemed to be an impossible feat, for there were twigs and briars everywhere I looked. I finally got tired of worrying about it and just walked through it as best I could. The sun was now almost down, and the moon had not quite begun to peek its head out, so it was getting rather dark. I tried to remember if it was time for a full moon. I sure hoped it was.

It was then that I saw a clearing just ahead and thought perhaps this would lead me to a trail of some sort that would carry me directly to the thicket I now felt compelled to see. My feet were guiding me every step of the way. I stepped out into the clearing, and my feet sunk into the years of dead pine needles below me. I gasped at the beautiful sight I saw before me.

It was as though the forest closed behind me like the curtains on a Broadway play, and the sun came back out as if the lighting for that Broadway play was installed way out there. The lighting on my face was brighter than I can ever describe. It was almost magical. Right in front of me I saw the smallest waterfall one could ever imagine. It looked like something some delicate homemaker would put on her coffee table. The soft trickling soothed me like a warm bath after a hard day at work, and I was being drawn to it. I wasn't fighting it, yet I wasn't really moving any muscles either. I was just gliding towards it. It was the most awesome feeling to experience my body moving without help. Before I knew it, I was standing before the small waterfall and listening to its flowing water.

Now this is where it gets hard to fathom, but I'm telling you that I was as much in disbelief as you will be, but it is a real occurrence that took place out there. As I gazed into the water that fell so perfectly from the small rocks at the top, I saw a face appear in the rocks behind the falling water; and although I never saw its lips moving, I heard it speak to me. I'm telling you, I did.

"Miracles only happen to those who believe, and you have been chosen." The voice was emanating from all over the forest, yet it wasn't very loud.

"I have been chosen for what?" I asked the thing that didn't move its lips.

"Your enjoyment of life in the simplest way has pleased the One that is greater than all. You have enjoyed His daily gifts of nature, and you have allowed yourself to dream of things that seem impossible. And the One who is the greatest of all wishes to reward you so that the impossible can be yours."

I laughed out loud at this silly thing before me. I was certain I would be found there in the forest laughing my brains out and would be carried away to the asylum down by the road. I had never been there, but the stories I'd heard were atrocious.

Then it spoke again. "You laugh because you were led to believe that there is no such thing as miracles. Your people scoff at those who do believe and have pushed many others away from being chosen themselves because of their cruelty to them. You must follow the path on your right to the window that has been set there for you. I will talk with you again."

The face disappeared, and I felt the last remnants of my laugh fade from my face. I rubbed my eyes and thought that perhaps I had been working too hard. I would forget the thicket and go home immediately. I turned to walk away and noticed that there were briars consuming the area in which I had entered this little garden of Eden. There was no way I was going back out *that* way. Then I saw the trail to my right and knew that that trail would be the only way for me to travel for now. *What had he said? To look through the window that had been set there for me.*

As soon as my feet hit the path, I heard the *click, click, click* and *jangle, jangle, jangle* again. It was much louder than it had been on the old dirt road, and once again my curiosity rose. As I drew nearer and nearer to the window that I could now see, I could hear the noise become denser. More sounds were mixed with it, too. It was not the type of window I imagined I would find, but it was a logical window under the circumstances.

I walked up to the image that was before me and stared. It looked as though it was a small cave atop a bunch of briars, and there was a dark smoky looking piece of glass in front of the opening. It looked like perhaps there were iron bars running down from inside of it. My first instinct was that this was not a *good* window, but I had nothing to base that on; so I bent over just a little to peer inside.

I heard clicking, jangling and moaning. Yes, I said moaning. It was louder than one could imagine, and people were in there! Some were hammering at stone walls; others were wailing, and they looked like they were in such distress. I was about to pull my head out from the atrocity I was staring into when I heard my father's voice.

"Now you listen to Him, boy. If you don't, you'll find yourself like your mother and me. I'm telling you boy, you had better listen."

I stuck my face to that window so hard that my nose began to hurt and the wound on my forehead began to bleed again. I had to look inside. I had to see if I could identify the person who was playing this practical joke on me. I didn't take too kindly to anyone playing games with me regarding my Pa. Obadiah Simpson may have liked his liquor, but he raised me to be a decent boy, and because of that, whoever was doing this was going to answer to me.

It was then that my heart slid down to my feet, and I thought for sure that I might die. It was my mama! She was looking at me with blank empty eyes, and tears rolled down her cheeks. Her color was pale, and it looked as though she were not my mother but perhaps some sick sort of replica of her. Then I heard her voice, and I knew that *this* was real. It was real, and I didn't want to know about it. Sometimes I think being in the dark is okay, and I would have rather been in the dark than to discover what I was about to discover.

"Jacob, you must heed the face you saw. Your father didn't listen, and I too chose to walk away from what was requested of me. You must do this, not just for yourself but for the people of Essex County, too. You can change things. You can bring them peace and joy. You just have to stand firm when they laugh and ridicule you. Do you hear me, son?"

"Oh Mama!" I screamed, running my fingers down the window, "Did they get you too? How can I get you out, Mama? Where is the door?"

"It's too late for me," she cried, "but you have been chosen to bring peace to Essex County, and you can do it. You just have to believe! Remember the day that you came home and told me that you had seen Robbie Jones running from a bush that was on fire?"

I nodded my head as the tears poured from my eyes. I remembered Robbie Jones. He was the little boy who told the town about miracles. He told everyone who would listen, and he was laughed at wherever he went in town. I had halfway believed Robbie because I had seen the bush from the tree I had been sitting in. I went down there the next day, and the tree was rooted there like nothing had ever happened to it. It wasn't long after that that Robbie went away, never to be seen or heard from again.

"Yes, I remember Robbie. What does he have to do with me?" I asked in bewilderment. I hadn't thought of Robbie since that summer long ago. What could he possibly have to do with this?

"Robbie talked of miracles, but he never found the words he needed to share it correctly. The answers, Jacob, are in a book next to my nightstand. You must read the book. You must let the truth be known. Don't let the town sway you. Stand strong and know the book," she said to me as a dense dark fog began to rise, obscuring my view of her.

The window was disappearing. Vines began to grow over the doll house-sized stone cave that contained the windowpane. As the vines grew, large thorns began to spurt from them, and I drew quickly back from the frame that was disappearing fast. Within another second, it was as though it had never been there.

"Mama!" I screamed, "I don't understand. Please don't leave me! I need your help with this. I can't do it alone!"

The sound of birds from far away is all that I could hear, and there was no sign of a window ever being there. I fell to my knees and cried. I was frightened and more than confused. I was certain I would be in the asylum by morning. I wished for my mother's sweet arms to once again surround me, but I knew that what I had seen was not of this earth and that my mother was dead. She had died in a car accident coming home from the bar in town. I didn't want to think of where she might be now. If that place *was* any indication of where she might be, I would have to find some other alternative to rest my remains.

I headed down the trail that I had traveled earlier, hoping that this unbelievable nightmare would soon end. I saw the bright light and followed it. Just as I expected, the face was behind the rippling water again. Nothing had changed. It still bore no expression on its face, and its lips never moved.

"You have been chosen. You will receive power from the greatest One of all. Your faith must be strong, and you must fight a good fight. Let not the evildoers destroy your dreams. Everything is beautiful in its own way. You know this already. Be off now and carry your suit of armor."

"Where is my suit of armor?" I asked. Something was telling me that I was going to need a suit of armor and probably a few other things as well.

"Seek and you shall find," It said to me just before disappearing again.

The rest you can probably imagine. I got through the thicket, hobbled my way home, and searched for the book my mother had left behind. I began to read that book every day as often as I could, and things really began to change. The townspeople laughed me out of town meetings and scoffed at me in the street. Yet they were coming up to me privately and asking how they could get "the power." I would hand them a little Holy Bible (I had purchased a hundred of them with my life savings, right after the—you know—and then I'd tell them to read it.)

Recently the people of Essex County built a little church in the courthouse circle and restored an old one down off the highway. They both are in full use now, and I've heard talk about them building another one. The most interesting part of this whole story is that they meet once a week now to give testimonies on their *miracles*, and when you drive past the church near the courthouse, there's a sign out front that reads: TRUE MIRACLES AWAIT YOU.

I found out what happened to Robbie Jones. There was a news article in my mother's Bible. It said that Robbie had taken his own life after going insane. He had seen a burning bush and tried to tell people about the truth that the bush supposedly had spoken of. He would go back to that bush and worship it when people started getting real hard on him.

I know that Robbie Jones didn't go insane. I believe that he saw the burning bush. He just didn't know where to find his answers to the truth he sought afterwards. He didn't know about the Book. Without the Book and his suit of armor, he could never have been strong enough to deal with the rejection the townspeople showed him.

As for my mother, I am grateful that she somehow managed to direct me to the Book long after it was too late for her. And as for the Book, I read it; and I have the suit of armor now. If you'd like one too, I suggest you read the Book.

Philipians 4:13: I can do all things through Christ, which strengthens me.

Matthew, Luke and John

*H*is receding hairline openly displayed the lines on his curled brow, and the wrinkles suggested that he carried much tension along with him. I never really thought much about that wrinkled forehead until today. I never really knew what it meant until just now. It had often scared me since he never looked happy when he wore those deep lines, and I was sure that he was always searching for something to find wrong with me. He was quite the serious type, and often I found myself just not liking the man. There was no particular reason; I just didn't like him.

He had met my mother when I was only seven years old. I think he laughed a lot back then; I can just vaguely remember that. The first time I met him, Mom had said that someone was coming over to take us to the fair on Saturday. The excitement I had felt from discovering that *I* would get to go to the fair brought forth many questions. Mother was laughing as she explained, displaying that shining smile she always wore when she was having a good day.

When someone finally knocked at our door that early Saturday morning, I raced to the door as quickly as I could. Mother was right behind me, scolding me for not announcing to her first that someone was at the door. It was a no-no to go to the door without Mother knowing it. She spoke quickly and then looked up at her guest with a smile that I had not seen before. It was a nice smile, but it had made me uncomfortable somehow.

There he stood at the door. He was smiling like I had never seen a man smile. Then he stepped through the doorway and stared into my mother's eyes for what seemed like forever to me.

"You look more beautiful today than I have ever seen you look," he said as he took my mother's hand in his and kissed it lightly.

My mother's eyes were sparkling when she answered, "Why, you look very handsome yourself, Matt." Then she looked down at me with her crystal eyes and placed her hands on my shoulders as she continued, "This is my son, Luke."

He knelt down on one knee and held out his hand. "Hi, Luke. I have heard so much about you. Your mother says you're a fine young man, and I can see that you do a wonderful job taking care of her."

"Thank you" was all that I could manage to get out as I shook his hand. I was beginning to feel like I didn't much want to go to the fair. Mother and I could have stayed right at home and had a picnic in the yard; we didn't need to go to any dumb old fair. But we went anyway. I wasn't about to tell Mother that I didn't want to have fun with her and her friend. She wouldn't have listened anyway. After a quick lecture on how rude I was being, she would have just said, *Now go get in the car.* There was one thing about Mother that I found out early: if she said she was going to do it, she was going to do it.

Ever since I was a baby, my mother had worked and managed to cook breakfast and dinner for me every day. I was proud of her for that. She would stand at the door and wave goodbye, saying, "I love you! Have a good day!" Some days I'd wonder if she really meant it. Still, she never let a morning go by that she didn't send me off that way. I would have to wait for her to get home in the evenings, but she never got home late. Tuesday was family night, and we would read verses from the Bible and talk about them. Mother would always apply the verse we read to my own life. She would say how God told her to read each particular verse to me. I often wondered how God knew what to write about each week. *Mother must have told Him in her prayers.*

Matt became a familiar face around our house. He would fix things that had been broken for years. I didn't really like that at first, but I didn't mind it when he found the old train set up in the attic and fixed it. Mother had always said it was my grandfather's, and by the grace of God she was going to see it running again for me. God sure did have a funny way of getting things done. *I would have rather thanked anyone but him for fixing it.*

It was right after school one day in fourth grade that Mother had picked all of her beautiful roses and placed them in vases throughout the house. The sweet aroma of her grand meatloaf was floating in the air like it had been sprayed from a can of air freshener. The dining room table had a new white cloth on it, and there were some long candles burning brightly. I had never seen anything look so beautiful. Something special was getting ready to happen, and it looked like it might be a party! I had never been to one, so I could only imagine how grand the evening would be.

After a search through the house, I found my mother trying on a dress. All of her other dresses were thrown across the bed, and the hangers were all cluttered together on her doorknob. She had her hair done up in some kind of fashionable bun and looked prettier than I had ever seen her before.

She looked up at me and said, "Hi, honey, did you have a good day?"

"Sure," I said. "What's going on here?"

"I have a special surprise for you tonight. I want you to get your Sunday school suit on and be at the dinner table promptly at 6:00. Okay?"

"Sure," I said, curiously wondering what kind of surprise would require my suit.

Dinner was wonderful! Mother had outdone herself this time. I was anxious to know why Matt had joined the two of us. We were sitting around the table in the dining room and I was just about to ask when Mother brought out her chocolate strawberry supreme. It was my favorite! As we began to dive into our dessert, Matt interrupted the most beautiful evening I had ever known.

He cleared his throat and looked me straight in my eyes and said, "Luke, your mother and I have known each other for some time, and I would like to marry her. I would like to do it with your approval. You both mean so much to me, and I would like to try to be a father to you. How would you feel about that?"

At that moment, the room began to spin. I didn't think that I would be able to eat my beautiful chocolate strawberry supreme. In fact, I think Mother's meatloaf was beginning to rumble in my stomach and was looking for a way out. *How dare he sit at my mother's table like that and ask me such a question*? What was I to do now? Telling him how I really felt would surely have gotten me the whipping of a lifetime, but welcoming him into the family wouldn't have exactly been tops on my list of what to say. So I did what I had to do.

"My mother has never told me that she was considering marrying you, and I think that would be more her decision than mine. Don't you think that you should ask her?"

Mother's brow began to curve, and that was never a good sign. She stared down at her plate as she responded, "Luke, I have already said yes to Matt, but we wanted you to feel a part of this union. Matthew is already such a big part of this family, and we just want to make it complete. You know, with a mother and a *father*."

What was that kick they were on about a 'father' anyway?

"Well, if you want to marry him Mom, you should do it." I said afraid to tell her what my true feelings were.

Dinner ended, and it was final. Matt would be moving in.

I often had wondered what having a father would be like. I didn't really mind that Mom had raised me. She told me very early on that my daddy was not around, nor would he ever be. My father was an *assailant,* and someday I would understand what that was. "But it's all okay," she would say, "cause I love you enough for both of us."

In the seventh grade, I came home one afternoon and slammed the front door. I trod up the stairs making as much noise as one teenage kid possibly could. I fell on my bed face first and let the tears roll from out of my eyes onto the soft blue comforter my mother had bought for me the year before. *Why didn't I have a father? Why couldn't I just be a normal kid?* There were things I needed to know, and I had no one to ask. The knock that came to my door at that moment still sends goose bumps up my spine.

"Luke, let me in. I need to talk to you." It was Matt, and he probably wasn't very happy about the door slamming. I wouldn't have been surprised if there was a little mud on the stairs since I had not wiped my feet.

I quickly wiped the tears off my face and fixed my hair. I opened the door just a crack at first. I had thought it better to see the look on his face before letting him in. The look I stood before was not at all what I expected. His forehead was not wrinkled, and he had a peaceful look about him.

"I just wanted to talk to you about the father and son baseball game that's coming up in two weeks. I thought maybe we could go as a team. There's a lot of talk about it, and I think that's where all the fun is going to be. I hear the mothers are even going to have a cookout at the park right after the game is finished. Would you mind honoring me as my son this coming Father's Day?"

The tears came harder than I have ever known them to come in my life. I fell into his arms, and I think I mumbled something like *yes, I'd like that.*

That was twenty-seven years ago, and today I still remember all the things Matthew did for me.

Today, I watched my first son be born, and I realized the preciousness of life in a way that was not familiar to me before. I realized that the assailant who raped my mother was not important, and I realized that a father comes from within. My father was not the man who followed my mother home from school when she was a senior.

He was the man who walked with me along life's way. He was the one who honored my mother, wisely carried us to church each Sunday, and showed me where I would find peace in my heart. He was the man who let my mother stay home and be with me after years of my watching her work hard to support me. My father is the man who stood here with me today as I watched my son be born into this world. He will be known only as Grandfather by my son, John.

On my twenty-first birthday, I changed my last name to Thomas. I am officially Matthew's son. I understand the wrinkles in his brow now. I think I see them in my own forehead. It isn't going to be easy raising a son, but I think I'll do it the way my father did, with lots of love and understanding. I'll love his mother the way my mother was loved, and above all, I will take him to church each Sunday so that he, too, will know the power of love.

Little Nelly

She had a contagious smile and her laughter was so loud and explosive that you could find yourself laughing with her and not even know what it was that she had you laughing about. She wore long baggy dresses that made her look years older than what she was, and she wore her hair up in one of those honey buns that you don't see too often anymore. Her old wool socks were wrinkled near the ankles, and they were snuggled by black boots that laced up in the front. She got an awful lot of attention wherever she went. She was considered the best *catch* in town, although she had little interest in men. But the thing that one would remember most about her was not her beauty or her infectious laugh, but the love that she showed for everyone with whom she came in contact.

Most of the times that I would see Little Nelly, she was toting her black Bible under her arm. She was either heading to the local convalescence center or off to read to the underprivileged. It looked as though her arm had grown used to the book being clutched underneath because whenever she was talking, she could still wave her hands around without the book budging. I never saw her in a bad mood or even in a neutral mood when she was out and about. She always displayed that happy face of hers in public. She was happy—at least as far as anyone could see from the outside looking in.

In the fall of 1974, I discovered that Nelly Brown was something special. Everyone knew she was special, but I doubt anyone knew just how special she was to me. Her sweet and kind ways had earned her great respect in our town, and often one would hear rumors about how Nelly Brown was really an angel sent from God to get people to treat each other kinder. She always seemed to be close by when someone was in need. I now know why she was sent here, and I do believe with all of my heart that she *was* sent here. My life took on an entirely different meaning after Nelly Brown entered it.

Joe and Glenna Brown had found Little Nelly on their front doorstep when she was only hours old. They had been trying for years to conceive a child, but with no success. So there was no discussing it when Glenna found Little Nelly outside her front door. She swore that the little girl was sent from God, and there was no way anyone or anything was going to take that precious baby out of her hands. They say that even the judge cried at the hearing from the pleas of Glenna Brown that day, and he decided without even taking the ordinary recess to give Little Nelly to them.

That's just the beginning of a long love story. The town watched Little Nelly grow up like she was one of their own. The media had focused so much attention on the little one's arrival that there was hardly anyone in town who didn't feel like they knew her. The townspeople watched as she took her first steps and then a few years later as she played hopscotch in the front yard of the Brown's little cottage. Then with awe, the whole town watched Little Nelly Brown become a beautiful, petite young woman.

She would hold her head sideways when she walked, and it gave a look of innocence that is indescribable other than to say it made you want to hug her. She would grab hold of the sides of those long baggy dresses she wore and tiptoe in a way that would make you think of a poised ballerina on one of those jewelry box pedestals that spins around when you open the box. She had no need for makeup; her beauty came from within and radiantly beamed outward. I have to admit it. I too was quite captivated by Little Nelly's charm.

I used to watch her walk past the house each morning as I would sit at the breakfast table and stare out the window while having my morning coffee. She would float down the sidewalk holding up her skirt and humming sweet hymns that she had learned at church. It gave me such a peaceful feeling each morning to watch her glide by. Then I would watch as she'd turn up the church sidewalk and graciously step up the six concrete steps out front to go inside. She would usually stay about half an hour, and then she would come out with her beautiful smile beaming as though she were expecting someone to be waiting behind the door when she opened it.

One particular morning as I sat by my kitchen window watching, I noticed Little Nelly was not quite as perky as usual. She still had her gracious glide, but some of the bounce seemed to be missing that morning. I watched her go into the church, and then I watched her come back out almost immediately. I couldn't tell for sure, but it looked like our Little Nelly was crying! What I was certain of was that she definitely was not wearing that beautiful smile I had never seen her without. I watched sympathetically as she walked down the sidewalk and turned into the old graveyard behind the church. I rose up and grabbed my jacket from the back of the old wooden chair in the kitchen, deciding that I would have to check and make sure that Little Nelly was all right. Taking one final gulp of my coffee, I sat the cup gently down on the old green kitchen placemat and walked outside.

The morning was a fresh autumn one. The leaves were all multicolored on the branches, and those on the ground were brown and crackling under my feet. The mist from the cool morning had not lifted, and it gave the entire atmosphere a spookiness about it that sent a chill down my spine. I pulled some of the cool air into my lungs and felt somewhat revitalized. I thought that perhaps I should start walking every morning; the fresh air would have done me some good. Early morning hours alone on a beautiful fall day seem to offer the soul a peace that passes understanding. It's like having God invite you into the Garden of Eden for a while. There were no sounds of manmade technology in the air—only a few birds that had gotten an early start at chirping their melodies. I wondered what I would find Little Nelly doing when I got inside the cemetery.

The rusting iron bars that hovered over the entrance needed a coat of fresh black paint. Cemeteries are never warm and inviting, but just a little neglect can make one look quite eerie. I walked under the iron lettering that read "Pine Grove Cemetery" and found myself wondering if the sky would turn black and half-dead corpses would start coming from out of the ground after me. I grinned at the thought. You could really let your imagination run wild out there. I let my eyes wander over the headstones and statues that lined the grounds. I saw no sign of Little Nelly. The morning fog was quite heavy. There were several places that I could not see where she could have been, and I figured I had better check those areas out just in case she had found herself in some trouble.

Something guided me around a big stone building that cemeteries sometimes put out in the middle of all the graves to house dead bodies in above ground, and I found myself wishing I was sitting back in front of my warm cup of coffee at my old kitchen table. That's when I heard her. It sounded to me as though she was crying, and yet I couldn't imagine that in my head. To see Little Nelly's face with anything but a bright vibrant smile was beyond imagining. I felt as though I should turn around and leave her here alone with her grief, but I couldn't bring myself to do that. This was Little Nelly—the girl who had brought so much to joy to people's lives—and for the first time that I had ever known about, she was in need of that joy herself.

I peeked around the back of the old stone building and saw her kneeling before a statue, talking through her sobs. The concrete man hovered over her several feet. He had his hands outstretched on a cross, and his face was carved to express great pain. He was clad only in a garment that was wrapped around His groin, and his feet were tied together. I recognized this as a depiction of the crucifixion and wondered why Nelly had found herself kneeling here before the statue's feet. God forgive me, but I listened to her speak to that statue through her sometimes inaudible prayers.

"I cannot talk to him, Father. He hardly knows who I am, Father. It's like I am so close to him and yet so terribly far away. How can I help him to know You, Father? Please send something this way that will open his eyes. He is my father even if he doesn't know me. I ask that You give me the opportunity to let me introduce him to You. Please hear me, Lord." She then began to sob, and I could not understand what she was saying. I felt the guilt of my intrusion building up inside of me again and thought briefly about turning back when I heard her speaking clearly again.

"Father, if it is Your will, then use me to save my dad. I will give all that I have to bring my father safely into Your hands. I praise You for all of Your greatness. In Jesus' name I pray. Amen." She stood and looked up at the face of the stone monument, clasping her Bible in both hands. I could not see the streaks of tears on her face, and yet I knew that they were there.

I suddenly had a rush of consciousness sweep over me and decided I should leave and leave fast. This was something Nelly had to settle with God and her father, and there was no place for me in it. Or was there? I hated when my brain would start ticking and dreaming up messes I could get myself into. Something told me that God had allowed me to hear this for a reason, and I was suddenly on a mission to figure out why.

My feet carried me quickly back around the stone building and out from under the iron sign at the front gate. Back home, I let myself in through the garage and headed straight for the coffeepot. I needed another hour or two in front of my kitchen window. The time that I spent there gave me plenty of opportunity to think and figure things out. I grabbed my cup from off the table and filled it, placed my jacket on the back of the wooden chair, and sat down to see when Nelly would leave the graveyard. I didn't have to wait long.

She stepped out of the entranceway with that cute little gait of hers, wearing that beautiful smile that I now knew was not as peaceful as it appeared. Her Bible was tucked neatly in the usual spot, and as she turned to go into town I watched her small frame disappear over the horizon. I continued to ponder how I might help Little Nelly with her heavy burden.

Joe Brown was a friendly enough fellow, but he seemed to be firm and set in his ways. I only knew him because I lived down the street from him. He worked in the courthouse doing something with water and utilities, and I owned my own construction business that required me to travel often, so there wasn't much opportunity for us to run into each other. We did wave at one another when we crossed paths on our street, and we talked about our yards when we did meet by chance on the sidewalk that runs through our neighborhood.

I had no idea how I could help Joe Brown, but I felt compelled to try and find some way to help open his eyes to his daughter's wishes. Joe Brown was the only father Nelly had known since finding her on the doorstep, and somehow he had to be told about his daughter's wishes. I wasn't in much of a situation to recommend that anyone go to church. I believed in God and often talked to Him in front of my kitchen window, but I probably didn't know enough about Him to be telling my best friend about him—much less someone I hardly knew. I wondered how I would even approach it. *'Hey Mr. Brown, have you met Jesus yet?'* or *'Hey Mr. Brown, do you know what your little girl wants more than anything?'* That didn't seem quite like the best kind of approach.

I sat there at the table for most of the morning wondering what I could do to help Little Nelly. I had come up with plenty of ideas, but none of them were very good. I reached across the table onto the counter beside it where I kept my notepads, sticky pads and bills. I began looking for a pen, and as I did so a light green envelope fell from out of the plastic mail holder I kept filled on my counter. I picked it up to put it back in the pile of envelopes when I noticed that it was my utility bill. That was it! I would go to the utility office in town and pay my bill. I wasn't sure where Joe Brown worked there, but there was a chance he ran the front office.

Rubbing my chin, I decided I could use a good shave before going, so I went into the bathroom to get ready for my little venture to the town courthouse. As I stood before the mirror that morning, I questioned myself on my actions. I hadn't cared that much for anyone else whom I had passed in this lifetime. I had never married, and I knew that was because I couldn't give of myself what women wanted. They enjoyed sitting around and talking about feelings, and I always had a job to do. Feelings weren't really my strong point. Maybe if I had had the kind of admiration for a woman that I had for Little Nelly, I would have married years ago. *What was it about that child?*

My face was all clean-shaven and smelling of Old Spice when I walked out the side door and through the garage to the sidewalk that led into town. I could have driven, but the early morning walk had revitalized me enough so that I thought perhaps the late morning breeze might offer me the same sort of comfort. I passed only a few cars as I walked the first two blocks, but as I carried on with my stroll the street became busier. I was on the fifth block when I heard the squealing of tires up ahead. I could visualize a fender bender of some sort from the sound of it, and I stepped up my pace so I could become one of those rubbernecks you see passing by whenever there's an accident. I wasn't usually one of them, but I also wasn't usually standing close by it when it happened.

I could the see the traffic begin to back up, and then as I drew nearer I could see a crowd of people in the street standing in front of an old blue farm truck. I began to nudge through the mob to see if I could help whomever it was who was in need. Someone asked, "Is there a pulse?" And then someone asked, "Has anyone called her father? He's right across the street at the Utilities office." I crept closer, thinking the whole time that someone else had to have a father that worked at the Utilities Office besides Nelly. It couldn't be her who was lying on the ground in front of that old blue piece of tin junk.

"Noooo!"

The wail that came from my mouth surprised even me. I saw her lying there on the black tar like a crumpled up doll. Her head was twisted, and her Bible was lying open on the pavement just a few inches away from her feet. Her tiny frame seemed even smaller as she lay at the feet of the spectators who were increasing in number with each passing moment. I wanted to scream at them all and tell them to go home and get away from the small girl who no longer seemed to be with us. But all that I could do was to bend down and cradle her tiny head in my lap as I sobbed like a child.

The paramedics showed up, and I vaguely remember someone telling me, "Sir you're going to have to let go of her now." I felt them tug my arms loose, and I watched as they carted her body to the wagon that I was certain waited to carry her to the county morgue. I saw Joe Brown looking on at the rescue squad with red swollen eyes and sunken shoulders that barely seemed to hold up his head. I wanted to run to him and shake him. *Why was he just standing there?* I wanted to chase the ambulance that was pulling off. *Where were they taking her?* I wanted to scream at the top of my lungs. This could not be happening.

Someone carried me to the hospital. I can't remember who. I only remember it being the longest trip I had ever taken. I walked straight up to the registration desk in the emergency room and asked to speak to someone regarding Nell Brown. The nurse immediately came from out of her circular booth and asked me to follow her. She led me to a room far down the corridor, opened the door, and waved me in. I let my feet guide me. I was tired, and I wanted to wake up from this nightmare. I wanted to go back to all of the mornings I had sat and watched Little Nelly. I wanted to see her sway by the house with her radiant glide, and I wanted to know more than anything why this was hurting me so much.

The room was decorated in bright yellow and orange furniture. It had a picture of a small white lamb and the question over it, "Where does your destiny lie?" I wanted to cry again when I saw someone move out of the corner of my eye. I looked to see Joe Brown sitting in a corner chair and holding a Holy Bible open somewhere in the middle. He had a certain kind of peace about him that I could not comprehend under the circumstances. It made me angry, and I thought that before the day was out I would leap at him with the rage and anger I felt boiling up from within.

He stood up from his seat and spoke words that changed my life forever, "I'm sorry I couldn't protect your little girl any more than this. I tried to bring her up right, and I think she blessed the heart of everyone she ever met. I know that you moved to our neighborhood so you could keep an eye on how we took care of her. I hope you approve, and I thank you for not telling her who you are. I know that must have been difficult for you." He hung his head, and I heard him sob briefly as he tried to hold it together in front of me.

My rage turned to pure shock in an instant, and I felt right at that moment, as people must feel who are losing their minds. "What on earth are you rambling about?" I asked him. "I moved to your neighborhood because I found a house I could afford there. I did not leave Nelly at your doorstep. If you saw me admiring her, it's because she was radiant and glowing. It was as though she was blessed by God Himself, and I am not the only one who has loved her. I am sorry if I made you think that she was my daughter. That was never my intention," I said to him, trying to iron out the confusion that dwelt inside this man's head.

"Oh, you didn't know? Nelly wasn't really left on our doorstep. My sister died giving birth to her. I put her on the doorstep just a few minutes before I woke Glenna up that morning. You honestly didn't know?" He looked at me quizzically as though he thought I was playing some sort of trick on him.

"I didn't know what?" I asked him, feeling a hint of aggravation rise to the surface.

"Nelly was your daughter. My sister was Elinor Chambers. Don't you remember her?"

My body froze, and everything went very black before I could speak. "Elinor was your sister? Well, why didn't she ever tell me she was pregnant? And what makes you think the child was mine, anyway? I only knew her for a few short months; and if she thought I was the father, then why didn't she tell me that?" I asked him, more angry and confused than ever.

"Elinor went to tell you the night she found out. I had taken her for the test and talked her into telling you. I took her by your workplace, and one of the men in your crew told her that you were at Barry's Bar. She asked me to take her by there. When she walked in, she found you in a corner booth kissing a red-haired lady. She ran out with tears streaming down her cheeks, ranting on and on about how you had used her and that she would never tell you about the child. I thought someone had told you when you moved in down the street from us. You mean to tell me that you never knew any of this?"

"No, I never knew any of it. I always loved watching Nelly and felt a certain kind of closeness to her that I could never explain, but I never imagined anything like this. You know, I watched her praying in the cemetery this morning, and she was crying and praying. She said that she wanted you to be saved. I was going to come and talk to you about it when I saw Nelly in the street." I drew the light green envelope out of my pocket and showed it to him. "She was hurting because you haven't given your life to the Lord," I said, trying to change the subject or perhaps pass on the shame that I was suddenly feeling.

"No, that wasn't me she was praying for. It was you. I had told her when she was fifteen that you were father because I was afraid you would do it before I had a chance to. She knew that you never attended church. So she would walk by your house every day to go to church, hoping that you would see her and praying that you would be saved through her faith and prayers. I'm sorry; I had no idea you didn't know."

I felt my knees buckle underneath me, and my body slid to the floor. My God, what had I done? Had I been walking through life so busy that I didn't stop to get to know the women I had been with? Did I miss the opportunity to raise a wonderful child like Nelly as my own because I was too busy? How painful it must have been for her to see her father across the street and to not even know him except for an occasional *"Hello, Mr. Murphy. How are you today?"* Oh, what had I done?

At that moment, the doctor walked through the door without knocking, and I found myself shuffling to get up off of my knees. He waited until I had gotten up and straightened my clothing before he spoke.

"Which of you is Nelly's father?"

I had to reply to that, "I would have known better how to answer that about five minutes ago, Doc, but I think it's okay if you tell us both." I looked at Joe who was nodding in agreement with me, and I felt truly grateful.

He sat down on one of the bright orange chairs and pulled his clipboard out in front of him before speaking, "Nell is a very sick little girl, and I can't tell you that she is going to make it. I can only tell you that if you have faith, you are going to need it." He went on to describe her injuries and how each one could be fatal. I only heard that she might live, and the rest of that time I spent silently praying to a God I barely knew.

We were allowed only a few minutes alone with her. I spent mine telling her how I hadn't known she was my daughter, but that I would never be far from her again. I received no response from the broken figure with tubes and casts covering her body, but I prayed once again that she would somehow know that I had been there.

As Joe and I left the hospital that night, we had little to say to one another. And yet I felt a bond between us. He had been the father I had not been to my little girl, and for this I would forever respect him. The sliding doors of the emergency entrance opened, and standing before us were hundreds of people burning candles and holding a prayer vigil on behalf of my Little Nelly. I mean, OUR Little Nelly was truly loved.

I looked over at Joe who was every bit as amazed as I was, and I said, "Look what a fine young lady you've raised. Everybody loves her!" He burst into tears, and I felt the urge to hug him and thank him for the wonderful job he'd done with my daughter. And right there before a whole crowd of people, I did exactly that.

It was about six months before Nelly got out of the hospital and another two years before she recovered enough to start teaching disabled children. She could no longer walk without a cane, so her radiant glide was gone, but the smile that she wears is even more glowing than before.

Joe and Glenna have been very kind about letting me be a part of Nelly's life. I participate in their holiday festivities, and they join me for cookouts. I have somehow managed to acquire a family life that I'm sure I do not deserve. And I gave my life to God before Nelly got out of the hospital. I had never known what that meant before. I realized that there had to be a God who let me discover the benefits of this beautiful girl I had not known as mine. I am convinced God put me in that cemetery to hear her prayer so I could do the right thing when I found out about her. She had told God that day that she would give her life for my salvation, and she almost did.

I now know what it is that captivated me so about Little Nelly. It was her eyes: I was looking into my own.

Ephesians 2:8: *For by grace are ye saved through faith, and that not of yourselves; it is the gift of God*

Suit of Armour

This story is true. To the depth of my soul, I tell you it is true. It sounds ridiculous to those who cannot imagine it, but I have this suit that protects me. It's a suit that you cannot see, yet it is more powerful than anyone could imagine. I wear it every day, and although it is invisible to the naked eye, I know it is there. This suit protects me and leads me into places that I would not dare go alone without it. It has brought me through so many different obstacles along life's difficult path. It doesn't make me look different, and it doesn't weigh me down. In fact, if anything it makes my load much lighter.

It was back in the spring of 1965 when I first heard about the suit, and I knew then that I wanted it or one just like it. I was walking home from school one day when I heard some chattering near the water's edge. Hoping to find some of my friends taking a dip in the creek, I took the path that would lead me directly to the swing rope that hung from a huge oak tree overlooking the shimmering water. I was about halfway there when I came across the chatter that had brought me on this course in the first place.

In the middle of the wooded area, I saw an old man talking as though there were a second party present. I could see nothing else around him. I couldn't help but try to draw nearer to see what was going on. It was then that I realized that there were definitely two voices, and yet I could only see one person. Doing my best to walk softly on the fallen leaves below my feet, I edged my way near the spot where the old man stood. He seemed to gaze straight ahead as he spoke. He did not make any hand gestures or movements that might suggest whether he was having a good conversation or a bad one. I know it was not my place to be listening to the conversation of a stranger—and certainly not to a conversation of someone who could possibly be insane. Yet the unusualness of it all seemed to make me want to investigate it further.

The old fellow had apparently built him a fire because I could see the flickering flames around his feet. The fire looked awfully close to where the old man was standing, but it must not have been too close since he wasn't dancing around or moving like his feet might be hot. Then I began to make sense of some of the chatter I had been hearing. His voice was now audible, and I could make out that he was in a very deep discussion.

He gazed straight ahead as he spoke, "You say that you can bring me gifts of this world that I may not be able to acquire myself, and for this I should cast down my suit of armor so that *you* can show me the way. But I say that you are a liar, and that as long as I am covered in my armor you are weak and cannot touch me. Your work is not more powerful than the One who gave me this suit, and of this I am sure." The old man spoke in a firm soft tone and showed no expression whatsoever.

Then I felt my skin crawl when the second voice spoke, "You think the suit you wear can keep me from penetrating your heart. Do you feel that you are more powerful than *I* am? You are but a mortal man who has little to show for his worthless life. Your family has deserted you, and you have only one true friend who is of little importance to this mighty world." The voice spoke in a way that was both thunderous and intrusive. I could sense something evil about the second voice—more evil than one could probably imagine. I knew that the intentions of this loud and disrespectful *thing* could not possibly be good, and I feared what might happen to the old fellow. Yet I could not see any fear in the old man's eyes.

"You are right that my friend has little importance in *your* mighty world, but I would be concerned if he did. What is important to you, Lucifer, has no value to me. As for my only friend, you are *so* wrong. For I have a friend whom you must already know, and He is much greater than you and all of your cheap tricks combined. He is why I have the power to stand here before you, and He is why you cannot touch me. My suit of armor will not let you touch my heart if I refuse to let you in."

The old man spoke with such confidence for someone who was talking to something great enough to be invisible and break sound barriers beyond belief. His gray hair made him look as though he had some age on him, and yet his skin was not wrinkled at all. I thought to myself that perhaps his age had not been hastened by worry. He appeared to be a peaceful man who was quite confident under the circumstances.

"I shall catch you when your back is turned! You will be weak and fall, and I will be much harder on you for your denial of me. You cannot walk through this world without my servants there to help me break you and make you fall. Your days will be miserable. I shall send trials on you often, and they shall get harder and harder until you no longer wish to live," roared the voice that made my skin crawl.

The old man was laughing now, and I feared that the evil voice alone would crush the hearing of the old man with its explosion of sound. "You *have* caught me when my back was turned, and I *have* faltered. But still you could not pluck me from the hands of the Almighty. You have sent trials my way that would send many men crying. What more could you do than to take my family away from me? What could be harder, you Evil One? I have walked through your trials and wished myself dead, but still you have not taken that which you cannot have freely. You speak of how you will devour me and yet you do not. Why is it that you do not? Is it because you cannot?" The old man's face was still gleaming with a joy that I could not comprehend.

"Your regrets shall come shortly," the evil voice wailed, "and you shall know true fear!" At that moment, bolts of lightening streaked from the sky and exploded on the ground all around the old man. He did not move. He did not falter, much to my amazement. The strikes continued, and thunder jolted my brain as I looked on at the unbelievable sight before me. And then the sky turned blue again and birds began singing merrily in the background as though there had never been an interruption in the atmosphere. I stood in awe as I watched the old man who was just standing there.

Then he lifted his hands towards heaven and softly whispered words that were not fully audible to me. I watched tears stream down his face and wondered why he had decided to cry now that it was all over. I thought of how I would have been running from the spot where he'd been standing and dodging lightning bolts like one crazy fool. And I don't think that I would have waited to start crying. That probably would have come first.

Moments passed, and the old man began to walk towards the trail that had brought me to this place. I could see that he was wearing one of those robe dresses that they wore back in the medieval days. I think they call them togas or something like that. I waited until he had passed the tree I had hidden behind before I came out from behind it. I didn't want to lose this guy. I thought it might be interesting to know who he was and where he kept his suit. Perhaps I would need that suit one day. I made sure I lagged behind him because I didn't want this guy who wore such a powerful suit to get angry with me. I waited until I thought for sure he was out of the woods, and I took off running to catch up with him.

The fresh air hit my face as I exited the trail, bringing me back to the world that I knew to be real. I looked for the old man and his wine-colored robe, but I saw no one wearing such attire. Just a couple of classmates and the school principal were walking back towards the school. Mr. Harris seemed to be in a hurry. His gait was rather speedy—more brisk than I had ever recalled before. He was a laid-back man whose wife had left him three years before. He had become even more of an introvert since that had happened. Rumor had it that he had become a hermit and had started a small church up on the mountain where he lived.

I was feeling a bit discouraged about losing the old man and decided that I would just go home and forget about stopping by the basketball courts. Louie and Ernie would probably wonder what had happened to me, but I just had too much on my mind to go mess around with those guys today. There was something about Mr. Harris that I couldn't seem to get off my mind, too. He hadn't looked the same to me, and I pondered what it was that was laying on my mind.

I began to whistle "When the Saints Go Marching In" to myself as I shuffled my way home. My father had always whistled that tune while he worked, and I had grown accustomed to whistling it. My mother had told me once that as a baby I had cried a lot, and the only way they could get me to go to sleep was if my dad came in the room and whistled that tune to me. I guess that's why I never looked for any other melody to whistle.

Well, I was whistling and thinking how gray Mr. Harris' hair looked as he had cantered towards the school. I hadn't realized how much my principle had aged. I knew that he was younger than my mom and dad because Mom always talked about dating his older brother Charlie whenever she was looking for my dad's attention. She never had any problem getting it like that.

That's when I stopped where I was and thought, *Oh, my goodness, that was Mr. Harris I saw in those woods. It had to have been. I knew it had to be Mr. Harris' gray head that I saw. But what would Mr. Harris be doing out in the woods wearing an ugly old toga?*

Mom sure was right about life getting more confusing as you get older because here I was only in the twelfth grade and I couldn't remember being more confused. I guess the only way I could find out the answers would be if I went up to that little church Mr. Harris had started up on the mountain. Then I wondered what I might say to my mother about going to church when she had such a difficult time getting me up to go to school each morning. I figured that she would be asking questions, and I had better have some good explanations. I decided I should tell her that I was studying suits, and I thought a good place to start would be in church. And if she persisted, then I would remind her that I did have a senior prom coming up. That would probably ease her curiosity.

The next day at school I asked Louie and Ernie to meet me at the public park a block away from school. Ernie realized something was up immediately because he looked concerned and asked, "Is everything alright, Vince?" I told him I would tell him after school, and we went about the rest of the day just like we normally did, shooting paper planes back and forth in Mr. Thomas' class each time he turned his back to write on the chalkboard and sitting with the basketball team at lunch. I couldn't keep my eyes off the clock the entire day, though; and when the time came for the last bell to ring, I didn't even bother stopping at my locker. I raced ahead of Ernie and Louie so I could stop by the trail to see if Mr. Harris might be back there. He wasn't.

Ernie and Louie approached me like their usual selves, giving cootie shot punches to the arm and calling each other names that I knew their mothers would wash their mouths out for if they had heard them. Louie was Italian and had those dark eyes that the ladies rave about in movie stars. Ernie was quite the opposite. He had pale skin and blue eyes, and his frail frame looked anorexic beside Louie's muscular one. The three of us were tight, though. We had all three been born in this small town in the same hospital, had gone to the same school, and even had the same teachers every year. We had other friends, but none of them could break the bonds the three of us shared.

I was eager to get started, so I held up my hands and said, "Hey guys, I need you to listen up." The breeze in the air seemed to give me some inspiration for sharing this most unbelievable tale.

They stopped their chatter and looked at me as I continued, "It's important guys," I said as I stood up from the wooden picnic table I had been sitting on while waiting for them.

I began to tell them about the event I saw take place the day before, and I couldn't tell if they believed me or not. But I didn't stop talking until I had gotten it all out. Then I waited for what seemed like hours before Louie broke the ice and said, "Well, when are we going to church?" And then they burst out in a chatter of plans and strategies. We decided that we would attend on Sunday, which was only a day and a half away.

We were about to head home when I stopped them. I had to ask, "You do believe me, don't you guys?"

Louie and Ernie turned around and looked at me. I knew they would tell me the truth, whether I liked it or not.

"Are you kidding, Vince? If anybody else had told us what you just did, we would have had a field day with it at school Monday morning. But we don't think you would go out of your way to make up something like this. Besides, if there is the slightest chance that we can get one of those suits you were talking about, we don't want to be left out on this one." Louie laughed, and Ernie followed along. I felt a little better.

Sunday finally arrived, and my mother didn't seem to be as curious as I had thought she would be. It was quite the opposite, actually; she seemed overjoyed. She offered to take us up the mountain herself, but I told her that Ernie was getting his father's car. She then went into her room and came out with one of my father's suits.

"You can wear this if it fits you," she said. "It's your father's, but he's only worn it twice. He says it has too many fancy gadgets for him. I'm sorry I haven't been out and gotten you one, son."

The suit had a nice red silk handkerchief in the top pocket, and the shirt that went with it had gold cufflinks at the cuffs. I couldn't imagine my father wearing it. He was so bland. "It's alright, Mom. I'm planning on buying one soon, so don't worry yourself over it." That statement was truer than my mother or even I knew at that time.

I put the suit on and was pleased at how well it fit for not having been fitted for me. I began wondering if I should start wearing one to school. I felt awfully sophisticated in it.

I could hear Ernie blowing the horn of his dad's old sedan out front, and so I kissed my mother and told her I loved her. Then I walked to the car as quickly as I could without appearing too anxious. Ernie and Louie were sitting in the car with their suits on. It made me feel a twinge of sadness because we were growing up. They no longer looked like my buddies to me but rather fine young men waiting to go out into the world. I jumped into the car, and Ernie pulled off blowing the horn as he drove out the lane.

We didn't talk much on the way there. Every now and then a joke about the suit was made, showing how anxious we all were. I could tell we were; it was in the air. I was glad that they had wanted to come, and felt relieved that I wouldn't be alone when I walked into this unfamiliar church we would be visiting. Slowly the car chugged up the mountain, and my mind wondered what would come of this day.

Once we were finally at the church, Ernie parked the old blue Chevy in the back where there were some spaces for parking. I guess there were about ten of them. Only three of them were filled, though, and the church didn't look quite like what we expected. It was a log cabin that had a log steeple running from the roof. There were three bells hanging from the rope in the center of the opening of the steeple. A wooden sign out front had been hand carved, and it read, *Sinners welcomed here.* It stood by the brown gravel that made a path up to the church's front door.

Ernie's face turned pale as he read the sign. He looked at me, then at Louie and said, "Gee, I hope these people aren't going to be walking in snake pits and all that stuff. I have *snakenaphobia*, and I don't think I can handle that."

Louie and I couldn't help but laugh at the *snaknaphobia* comment. Ernie was sometimes just a little too much. We laughed all the way up the pea gravel walk, and then we began to pull ourselves together so we could look like decent human beings (as my mother would put it) when we entered the church.

As we walked through the thick wooden door with the bronze handle, we were surprised to find no organ music playing and only four others sitting on the wooden pews. There were four lines of wooden bench-like pews, and two people sat on the front row of each side. The couple on the right looked to be in their early thirties, and the two on the left were a woman and a small boy. The little boy turned and tried to straddle the bench while his mother scolded him. He then turned back around.

Louie sat on the last bench on the left behind the lady and boy. Ernie stepped over the bench and sat next to him. I couldn't bring myself to do, that so I walked to the other end of the pew and walked back to sit by Ernie. I behaved as if it were the type of bench you'd find in any other church. I noticed that there was a peacefulness inside those walls, and I really didn't feel uncomfortable at all.

The altar was simple enough. There was no seating for a choir, and the podium wasn't much more than an old stick on a piece of board nailed to the top. And right next to the all natural podium was a single barstool with an old guitar leaning up next to it. Some hand picked wildflowers were in a vase on the stand behind the podium, and just above that was the prettiest stained glass window I had ever seen.

The sun beamed through, sending a colorful display of rays on the altar area. It gave its own lighting effect. The picture engraved in the glass was that of a knight kneeling beneath a ray of light and weep-ing. The ancient-looking calligraphy read, PUT ON YOUR WHOLE SUIT OF ARMOR. My heart raced, and my temperature rose. There was the perfect opportunity to ask someone about the suit of armor—the one with all the power!

Right then Mr. Harris walked out in front of the pews and picked up the guitar that looked as though it could have been his father's. He turned to look out at the small number of people before him, and our eyes met. He had seen me! I didn't know if I liked that too much. What would he think? Would he know that I knew about his precious suit of armor that he was keeping way up here on this mountain?

Then he spoke, "Good morning, friends. I see we have some guests here, and I would like to thank them for coming. Since there are only a few of us, perhaps we could stand and introduce ourselves. Would you like to start?" He gestured towards the couple on the right.

There was a slight pause, and the man stood up first. He looked like a lumberjack, a short replica of Paul Bunyan. I wondered if this was the only friend that Mr. Harris and the evil voice had been talking about. "My name is Carl Bowden, and this here's my wife, Luetta," he said in a mountaineer's drawl. His wife stood and quickly planted herself back down on the pew. She was stout and quite homely. Then the lady on the left rose, "My name is Virginia, and this is my son, Zebediah. I call him Zeb." Zeb began to wave and smile at us. Then his mother whispered something in his ear, and he sat back down.

Louie stood up first, then Ernie and finally me. I had thought it would be much more difficult, but even the guys said later on that they hadn't found it all that hard. The place was kind of inviting.

Mr. Harris sat down on his little bar stool and said, "I'm Howard Harris, and I'd like to get started with a song I have on my heart his morning. It's called, "When the Saints Go Marching In." Then he did a couple of practice strums on his guitar and began the melody I had become so accustomed to. I had never heard it played before on the guitar, but the sound was beautiful to me. Ernie and Louie seemed to be enjoying it, too.

After the song, Mr. Harris shared with us why he had opened the church. He explained how he saw children hurting every day. Their parents wouldn't talk to them, or one of them drank—sometimes both. He said he didn't realize how much people were hurting and being hurt until his own tragedy. He had been a workaholic and neglected his family; and because he didn't know God, he didn't have a chance at fighting with the evil worldly forces when his wife became fed up and left. He shed his tears with us, and before the sermon was over, Louie, Ernie and I had streams of tears running down our cheeks. I can't tell you exactly what all happened next, but I know that all three of us left church that day with our suits of armor.

We've built a much larger church now, and our congregation continuously grows. Ernie became a preacher, and now lives out in Georgia with his wife and three kids. Louie just got married last year. He's a missionary in India where he met a wonderful girl. I haven't met her yet, but he writes me often to tell me about her. We plan a reunion next year, right here on top of the mountain. I have a large ranch on the property next to the cabin, and I have built some small houses there so the homeless can work for shelter and an opportunity to get back on track. It's had a pretty good success rate so far.

Mr. Harris died last year, but he did reunite with his wife a couple years after he opened his little church. He praised God for it every time I ran into him after that. Zebediah is now the new church pastor. His mother, Virginia, met a nice man from town and married him about a year ago. She takes care of all the floral designs at church, and he is the youth pastor. It's amazing how things can turn out when you're wearing the whole armor of God.

And by the way, about that afternoon in the woods by the creek trail—Mr. Harris says it never happened.

Ephesians 6:11-13: Put on the whole armour of God, that ye may be able to stand against the wiles of the devil. For we wrestle not against flesh and blood, but against principalities, against powers, against the rulers of the darkness of this world, against spiritual wickedness in high places. Wherefore take unto you the whole armour of God, that ye may be able to withstand in the evil day, and having done all to stand.

The Perfect Example

I sat in the attorney's office, staring straight through his chubby little cheeks as he bounced around in his expensive leather swivel chair. He was chattering on and on about legalities, but I couldn't hear a thing he was saying. My mind was drifting.

The old white farmhouse still sits out in the midst of a huge soybean field. The long dirt road that leads to the house with green shutters and matching green window flower boxes that are now empty leads into a nostalgic view of the past. The first tractor that the farm ever purchased now sits in the front yard, surrounded by what was once a radiant display of flowers but is now overgrown with weeds. Some of the green shutters, faded by weather, are holding on by only one hinge; and the front porch desperately needs some boards replaced. But that old house gives me a feeling of warmth I cannot express in words every single time that I pass by it.

The old man who owned the house passed away last year. I called him "Arnie," and he was the closest thing that I have ever had to a family member. It's not because I was orphaned, either; at least not technically. I had both a ma and a pa, and they always kept a roof over my head and clothes on my back. They never let me forget it, either. They weren't so bad, I guess; it just seems that the day my brother Dale was hit and killed by a car while walking home from school, they went away with him.

Ma sat around and wept often, refusing to let anyone into the new world she had created around herself. Pa was dealing with Ma cracking up and my brother dying by drinking it all away. I don't believe I ever saw him sober after that. He even kept a small bottle of whiskey in his shirt pocket. Often times he could be found out at Sammy' bar and sometimes he didn't come home for days. Most of the time I found myself wondering if they knew that they still had me.

I remember just as if it was yesterday the first time I met the old man. It was several weeks after Dale's funeral, and I was feeling particularly sad that day. I couldn't bring myself to go to school; there was too great a chance that I would lose it in front of my friends. Having my friends give me a hard time about anything at that time probably would have been the straw that broke the camel's back. I believe that I could have slipped into my ma's world and experienced bliss in a whole new and different way. So I had veered off of the path that led to school and ventured through the woods that would lead me to a creek in the back of the old farmhouse property.

I had found comfort atop a tree branch that had grown sideways, forming a bench-like seat, and I had begun to cry. No, I didn't begin to cry. Actually, I began to wail. Each wail seemed to be louder than the one before, and each one seemed to release something that had built up inside of me. The pain of losing my brother was terribly great, and the sad realization that I had lost my parents, too, had begun to set in.

I didn't hear the old man come up behind me as I wailed at the top of my lungs in that tree. I sobbed like I was losing my mind, and it felt good in a weird sort of way. I jumped when his loud voice broke through my sobs.

"What are you doing on this here private property, boy?" I was so startled that I lost my balance and toppled backwards, landing at the old man's feet.

My eyes fell on the old boots he had on, the type made from leather that lace halfway up the front of his leg. They were caked all in mud and the leather was coming apart at the soles. It looked to me that it was definitely time to buy a new pair.

His bib overalls were faded and worn, and the old red handkerchief that hung from his pocket was raveling at the edges. It seemed to me as though that hanky would be thrown in the ragbag very soon along with the old leather boots he wore.

I was pushing myself up from the grassy moss I had fallen into when I felt my body rise up and land on my feet. The old man had offered me a kind hand by grabbing me by the back of my shirt collar and lifting me straight up onto my feet. I was so startled by this man's actions that I had to calm down my bladder before I could do much else. I was mustering up the courage to apologize when his loud voice burst through the air once again.

"What's the matter with you, boy? Have you been drinking Conway Long's moonshine and lost your mind or something? What's going on out here? It sounded like a band of Indians on a warpath!"

The words were pouring into my mind, but my mouth was having a hard time sending forth a message. Then finally some sounds began to come.

"I'm sorry. I thought that I was alone and...my brother died and...I feel really lonely, and I..." I burst into tears once again, unable and unwilling to hold it back. The man stepped forward and embraced me. He held me that way for the longest time, never saying a word.

Eventually I regrouped and began telling him everything that was happening in my life. We sat down on the bench-like tree branch that I had fallen from, and I told him of my brother's death and the way my parents were behaving. I even told him about my grades in school—how they were suffering, but my parents hadn't even noticed. I told him how I felt, and then I asked him if he had ever felt alone like that.

It was then that I noticed a softness sweep over the large man who probably stood at least six feet tall. His soft eyes were almost covered by his thick black eyebrows that curled downward, and his lips had begun to tighten as though he was very lost in thought.

"I feel like that most of the time, son," he said in an unsteady voice, gazing off into the unknown.

I turned and looked up into the old man's dark caring eyes, and once again I opened the dam of tears in front of the complete stranger. He embraced me in a fatherly way until I had quieted the uneven breath that was coming out of my lungs. I laid my head on his chest and asked, "Well, what do you do about it?"

He paused for a moment and then asked me in a voice that was barely audible to follow him and he began to walk away without waiting for an answer. I watched as he walked away from the tree branch and began to walk towards the trail that led to the old farmhouse. I didn't really want to follow him. I felt that I needed to go home and sleep some of my anxiety away, but I knew that the old man had an answer for dealing with great burdens. And more than anything, I needed to know what that remedy was. I hurt all over, and the pain had just recently started to creep up into my brain. The old man said that he knew that feeling of sheer frustration, and for that alone I felt a certain kind of closeness to him.

He led me down a narrow path that was cleared freely of briars and branches that sometimes swoop down and scratch the skin. I kept up a pretty fast pace, and still the man seemed to be getting further and further ahead of me. His stride did not seem rushed at all. He merely took one step for each of my two. I trotted along after him; something told me that I didn't want to get lost in those woods.

We reached the back of the soybean field and looked ahead at the old white house that stood freshly painted and landscaped perfectly. After walking with the old man for what felt like a mile, we were across the field and in the backyard of the beautifully landscaped property. I gasped at the sight before me. There was a gorgeously designed flower garden hedged in by huge railroad ties and several trellises that were overgrown with roses of all different types. There was an old wheelbarrow pushed up beside the outhouse that was decorated with irises along the side of it. And there were even flowers blooming forth from the wheelbarrow. I couldn't help but wonder how the man kept all of this looking so lovely.

He led me over a tiny bridge that spanned a small stream and led up to a stone path that guided us directly to the back porch door. The porch windows had plastic on them that had been rolled up to the tops of the windows. I could see some plants hanging from hooks that were screwed into the ceiling inside. He opened the door and walked onto the porch. There was a wrought iron table with a glass top, and around it were matching chairs. A crystal vase sat in the middle of it, and it was filled with beautiful multi-colored roses and a spray of little white flowers that obviously came from his garden. It was so inviting that I felt at ease almost the moment I stepped inside.

He led me through some old French doors that opened up directly into the kitchen. There were windows on all sides of the house, and the sun lit up the room like nothing I had ever seen. Plants were in front of just about every window, and most of them were sporting colorful blooming flowers. His iron skillets hung from a rectangular rafter in the ceiling, and he had a wooden table under it with a chopping board and a razor sharp knife sitting perfectly upright on it. An old black kettle sat on the wood-burning stove, beside which was stacked a neat pile of wood.

He stopped in the kitchen, turned around to look into my eyes, and asked me, "Would you care for some lemonade or tea?"

I had really wanted to say no, but I felt that it would be rude. I should not just come in and get his secret for dealing with life and then go, so I did the right thing. "Yes," I replied, "thank you."

He pointed at the shelf that held the glasses and then the old icebox. "I'll be waiting in here for you." He turned around and walked out of the kitchen.

I cautiously grabbed a glass from off of the shelf and wondered why the man just didn't have cabinets instead. The shelves were cute, and the plates and bowls were all stacked neatly on the wooden shelves that were made of dark cherry wood, but I would have preferred cabinets. I went to the old man's icebox to pour some tea, and I flipped down the handle to open the door. As I reached inside, I saw an old corsage still in the box and turning many different colors of brown, a glass pitcher of tea, a plastic container with lemonade, and some butter. I couldn't help but wonder why a rotten flower was sitting inside the cleanest icebox I had ever looked inside of.

I quickly made my drink and headed out the door I had seen Arnie go through. The lighting changed greatly as I stepped into a dark room that looked as though it had not been used in years. As my eyes adjusted to the darkness, I realized I was standing in the dining room. There were two doors in the wall on my right, and one that was built with an arch. It was straight ahead. I took the one straight ahead because the other two were closed, and I didn't think the man would close the door if he were waiting for me to find him. I stepped softly through into the old room with wooden slats in the floor. There was an old braided throw rug that laid underneath the table which looked as though it could open up to be much longer. The flowers that sat on the dining room table were a far cry from the beautiful arrangement on the back porch. These flowers were all wilted and dead. Dried petals were lying on the table around the bottom of the milk jug that had been used as a vase, and they looked as though they had been there for a very long time. The place settings for two were covered in dust, and the dinner napkins looked faded with age.

I walked through the circular archway and into the most heartbreaking sight I had ever seen. I was standing in the formal living room, and the furniture that beautifully decorated the room was hardly even noticeable. Sitting right in front of a picture window were two eight by ten black and white portraits of a very pretty lady and a small boy who was smiling and displaying the loss of his top two teeth. The first thing that saddened me about all this was the fact that there was a candle burning in the center of them, indicating to me that I was looking at a memorial of some sort. A huge Holy Bible was sitting on part of the window's wooden insert, and a small clipping about two deaths.

The first read, "Mabel Jane Simpson, age 29, departed this life on February 6, 1958. She is survived by her husband, Arnold Herman Simpson II. With her, she takes her precious son (please see below). Funeral will be at Sandridge Funeral Home at 7:00 p.m. February 9." The one below it read, "Arnold Herman Simpson III, age 10, departed this life on February 6, 1958. He is survived by his father, Arnold Herman Simpson II (Please see front local page). Funeral will be at 7:00 p.m. February 9, 1958."

I moved the clipping from off the top of the big Bible and opened the pages, finding the place where I saw a newspaper clipping sticking out. I know it wasn't my place to snoop, but I had to know what had happened to these two people. I thought that most assuredly they were Arnie's family members.

Then the old man's voice interrupted my thoughts once again that day. "They were killed in a bus accident. I had just gotten a new buyer for the soybeans and wanted to celebrate. Mabel was at her sister's, and I was supposed to pick her up. Instead, I decided to ask her to take the bus with Little A. That's what I called him. She hadn't been real happy about it, but I finally got her to agree. I went out and picked some of her fresh flowers, bought some steaks, and was going to throw them on the fire. I arranged for our neighbor, Miss Bessie, to watch Little A so we could go dancing afterwards. I sat and waited all night for that bus to show up, holding that stupid corsage I had bought her like a fool. It never did." His voice began to waiver as his eyes gazed ahead at something known only to him. I felt that he was telling me this because he had caught me snooping. I wondered if I should apologize, but he seemed to want desperately to tell his story. And I had a need to listen.

"It was about two in the morning, and I was getting ready to leave the depot and go look for them myself when two policemen approached me. They asked me my name and then told me that they had some terrible news for me. I could tell that they did not want to be standing in front of me, and I knew before they spoke that my family was gone—taken from me in a split second. My regrets were overwhelming. I should have picked them up myself. To this day, I cannot throw out the corsage I bought her. And the dining room has remained the same. I had picked those flowers for her fresh out of her garden. She loved them so."

He ceased talking and gazed at his unknown realm again. His shoulder was leaning up against the arched doorway, and it looked as though it were holding him up. I saw a small tear trickle from his eye, and I felt bad that I had poured out my problems onto him when he was suffering so much himself.

"I'm so sorry," I said to him with more sincerity in my voice than I had ever heard before.

He held up his hand and said, "Don't apologize. Realize when you're sad that you don't have to be, and realize when you have to be that it's okay to be. Trials sometimes have the tendency to make us stronger. Life isn't easy for anybody, but it seems like some of us get a worse load than others. We simply can't do anything about that. All that we can do is put faith in what works and walk each day with that faith believing that breakthroughs will come."

"Does it ever get better?" I asked him.

"Yes. It did this afternoon, when I found a friend who needs the answers to life as badly as I do. It happened when I heard you weep, and I knew that I could be there for you. Nothing ever takes the place of the things we lose, but we have to move on. We move on, and we allow it to make us better people. Can you understand that, son?"

I shook my head up and down, but I could not speak. He took my hands, opened them up with my palms displayed, and said, "Here are your answers, son." He placed the large Bible in my hands and looked me in my eyes. "Are you sure you want the answers?" I again nodded my affirmatively.

"Then we can find them together," he said as he embraced me.

I visited Arnie Simpson every day after school after that, and we studied the Bible together, learning a new verse each day. I learned a lot from that old man—things that will take me through the rest of this life and into the next, thank God.

"Mr. Casey? Do you hear me?" The question brought me back to the room. "I just need you to sign these two forms, and the old Simpson place is yours. I hope you don't mind restoring things, because it looks like you've got your work cut out for you."

"Oh, sure," I said. "Thank you, Mr. Feinberg."

I bent over and signed the deed of the house that Arnie Simpson had left me, and I headed out the door hearing Mr. Feinberg chattering as I exited. I drove to my little two-bedroom rancher and walked up the drive. Sally Ann was standing there with her beautiful smile, holding our precious six-month old son, Russell Arnold. I bent forward to kiss her soft forehead and nuzzle his tiny neck.

I thanked God for the moment, and I thought of no better place for planning a future than in a house where I knew love had dwelt—a place where misery visited but hadn't been allowed to stay. I thank God for the chance at happiness He has granted me. And through His goodness and mercy, I hope to console every broken heart I come across, just like the old man who made sure I knew where the answers could be found. I hope to be the perfect example for my son and all others I encounter through life's walk just like the old man was for me.

My family will move into Arnie's place in a couple of months. Sally and I will pour the love back into the beautiful landscaping and the old inviting farmhouse. We will live there and represent the family that Arnie lost much too early in life. And though Arnie is no longer here I will keep his memory alive by restoring his home the way he had it beautifully done for his family.

The old man who set the perfect example for a hurting lad will never be forgotten and perhaps someday in some way, I can return the wonderful gift I was given to someone whose loads are just too heavy to bear alone.

I Timothy 4:12: *Let no man despise thy youth; but be thou an example of the believers, in word, in conversation, in charity, in spirit, in faith, in purity.*

The Cast Iron Bell

*T*hat old red barn had sat there for as long as anyone could remember. It had more tales of oddities than any other place I have ever heard about. My friend Tommy and I had often tossed stones at the old iron bell that was attached loosely to the building as we walked home from school years ago. The barn received a new coat of red paint about every three years, and someone kept the grass from growing up too high around it. I never really knew who did it, but whoever it was did a nice job of hiding its age. The barn was a part of the town—a big milestone that marked the entrance into Locust Grove. It was an attraction to tourists and a quiet history to the townsfolk. I never knew how important that little barn was, though, until the night it burned down.

I had just gotten home from working at the *Locust Grove Review* and was walking through the door when I heard my telephone ringing. I was entering from the back door and was glad that I didn't have to run for the phone like I would have had to from the front door. I reached up to the yellow phone whose circular dial was covered in dark smudges from years of use. "Hello," I said into the phone with one foot in my sliding glass door and the other out.

The voice came blasting over the phone with such a force that I had to pull the receiver away from my ear, "Russ, you had better get over to the big barn down at the intersection. You know, the old Burns' place. There's a fire down there, and the people around town are saying it might get out of hand."

I was the local town journalist, and I got all of the big stories like barn fires and any other breaking news. That's about the extent of Locust Grove's newsworthy news. Sometimes I actually resented being disturbed at all hours of the night for simple things like a barn burning or a brawl out at Michael's Tavern, but the salary was good and I was thankful for what the good Lord had blessed me with.

"Don't worry about a thing, Doris. I'll go there right now. Any idea how it started?" I spoke into the old yellow phone.

"No word yet. I don't think the fire department has been on it very long. Need any thing?"

"Nothing," I said. "I'll be in touch." I placed the phone back on the hook and thought that perhaps my life would have been a little more exciting if I was to move to the city. There were lots of people living in the city, and places stayed open all night. Surely there had to be something bigger than a barn fire or cows blocking the road. I went to the kitchen and poured myself a glass of soda, grabbed a carrot from out of the crisper, and headed back out the door that I had just recently entered.

I could see the smoke billowing in the sky as soon as I pulled out on the main road that led through Locust Grove. It was a little over a mile from where I lived, and already I could see cars pulled over on the side of the road and people walking towards the huge billows of smoke. It looked as though the crowd was going to make this a mad house to get around in. There were probably people in this town who were born in that place (I chuckled to myself), and some of them would be hovering around bawling their eyes out over its demise.

I pulled my car up to the town cop who was trying to keep the situation under control, and I waved to let him know it was me, the town journalist. I only needed to carry my badge for places outside of the town. Everybody knew me around here. I was the *only* town reporter. There were three fire trucks pulled up around the intersection surrounding the barn, and they all had their hoses pointed in the air blowing out tremendous spurts of water. I was amazed at the number of people who were standing around with somber faces looking as though they had lost a dear loved one.

The blaze roared from the top of the barn in flames much larger than I had seen in most of the fires I'd been to around town. I didn't think that this barn had much of a chance from the looks of the situation at hand. The building was engulfed, and the hay inside of it was most assuredly accelerating the flames and working against all the hard work of the firemen.

I took out my old news camera that had the manual hand gadgets to get close ups, and I strung the old leather strap around my neck. I began to set the focus with all of the little knobs around the lens and zeroed in on the old barn. I looked through the lens and then brought the camera down to examine it. I looked ahead of me to make sure I was still standing in front of the barn, and I looked through the lens again.

I couldn't believe my eyes! Each time I looked through the lens, *it was there.* So what was I to think of it? Through the lens of my camera, I could see a little white church with the kind of steeple that had the opening for a bell. Hanging beautifully inside the hole was a bronze bell just as pretty as if it had been hung there moments ago. Beside the door I saw an unusual black cast iron dinner bell nailed to the right side of the front double wooden doors. I began to snap pictures of the scene in front of me, not sure if the film would show the barn or the church when they were developed. It didn't matter. I had to get as much footage of this situation as I possibly could. I knew that I wasn't going to be able to tell anybody about what was happening out there unless I had something to prove whatever it was that was going on because it didn't even seem real to me. I began hoping by some miracle of faith that I would get something on this camera that proved to me that I was not losing my mind.

I watched the sun go down as the firemen worked diligently to put the flames out. The now smoldering pile of wood was nothing more than black rubble with a dark cloud hovering over it. The firemen were packed on two of the trucks and ready to pull off while fire engine number three was rolling up the huge fire hose that ran from the bright red engine. It wasn't until I saw the last one's taillights in a distance that I realized what was taking place around me.

People were standing holding candles all around the front of the barn in the ankle high grass that had been cut with a bush hog and surrounded the old barnyard. They were humming the hymn "Rock of Ages." My mother often had sung it when she hung up clothes out on the line behind our house. I knew the song well. I wanted to sing right along with them, but I felt ridiculous. This was an old barn, for crying out loud!

Every now and then someone would cry out a verse that I would recognize as something I had heard in the Bible, and some of the others would call behind it, "Yes, Father."

My first instinct was to walk back to my brown sedan and drive off, leaving these people to do their thing. But the reporter in me would not allow that. Something else that I couldn't explain was keeping me there as well. I wondered if all this chanting had anything to do with the church I had seen through my camera lens. It seemed that I had heard a story of an old church being there once. I saw an old red ford truck pull up where fire truck number three had been parked, and I watched as an old man stepped from out of the truck he had driven up in. He wore hunting gear from head to toe, starting from the old camouflage cap he wore right down to the rubber camouflage boots ridiculously wrapped around the legs of his camouflage jumpsuit. I watched as he reached over the side of his truck into the back and pulled out a large cardboard box. Then the man in the hunter's coveralls staggered with the box over to the partially grass-covered drive where a large church wagon had parked without my seeing it pull up. It was the oldest wood-paneled wagon I had ever seen. It looked like it should be placed in some sort of auto collector's museum.

The people who stood around the burning embers began walking towards the man with the box. They stood around him as though waiting for him to place the box down on the ground so they could take what it was he had been toting. I watched as they bowed their heads and the hunter man led them in a prayer. This whole situation had become quite peculiar. After the man finished his prayer, he pointed to the box in front of him; each one of the people bent down and anxiously pulled something from out of the box. It didn't take me long to realize what it was. I looked on bemused as the candles were being lit before me. The man had brought a whole box of them, and it looked as though he might use every one of them.

The people congregated into nice even lines and sat Indian-style on the ground, staring straight ahead at the smoldering embers as they waited for something to take place. They even left a jagged row between them like an aisle of some sort. I was staring in amazement at the scene that was taking place before my eyes when the glare of headlights hit my face once again that evening. I turned to look at the faded beams and saw what looked like a model T Ford pull up and a little old lady who looked as though she were at least a hundred years old step out of the passenger side.

The people all bowed their heads and began softly chanting a song I could couldn't quite recall the lyrics to, and yet the melody was quite familiar: *Onward, Christian soldiers, marching as to war, with the cross of Jesus going on before…*

The voices of the people briefly faded out as I watched the elderly lady slowly move up the makeshift aisle in the center of the crowd, a cane guiding her course. She hardly seemed to have the energy to make it to the front, and yet she kept onward. *How fitting*, I thought to myself. She finally made her way to where the front of the barn once stood and waited for the singing to cease…*Like a mighty army moves the church of God; Brothers we are treading where the saints have trod; We are not divided; all one body we, one in hope and doc-*

trine, one in charity. Onward, Christian soldiers, marching as to war, with the cross of Jesus going on before!

I gazed up at the old lady who had reached the front and had now turned and faced the crowd. I could see tears streaming down her face. She looked up into the heavenly sky that was now decorated with more stars than I could ever recall seeing before. Then she raised her hands and waved them in a back and forth motion to the sound of the lovely hymn that was coming to a close. She may have needed her cane to walk, but she didn't need it to stand and sway. It amazed me. She seemed to have more energy streaming from those old bones than I would have ever given her credit for.

The singing ended, and I thought it sounded as though beautiful music had been sounding with the words of their hymns and had now stopped as well. The old lady cleared her voice, and I thought how she could have started coughing up cobwebs by the looks of her aged skin. Then she spoke in a voice that was much softer and more feminine than I would have ever anticipated.

"We are meeting here to say farewell to the old barn that we all know had so much more to offer than its breathtaking view that exists no more. Those of us who have been around long enough know that this old building was the town's second church. We know the troubles that we had to make it a home for the heavy-burdened, and we know the joy that it brought forth.

"My father, Zacharias Fitchett, was the pastor of this little church. And he warned me of the day that this building would fall. He warned me that without the faith that this building has brought forth in the people of Locust Grove, a great sadness would surely follow. We have secretly met here for over thirty-eight years now, and we know that the faith inside was much greater than anything we experience here on earth.

"My message to you tonight is: Don't let that faith slip away from us. We must hold onto our faith and bring back the building that has helped guide many of our brothers and sisters to salvation. Most of us remember the barn and hiding out from villains who sought to destroy us. If my father were here, he would remember the church—and even before that, the log benches and hand-carved podium that was once surrounded by woods here and was only a dream of a church. Regardless of what we remember about this building, we must remember Who lived within its realm."

The old lady paused, and for a brief minute I thought she would keel over right before my eyes, but she heaved in a big breath of night air and continued, "My time is short, and just yesterday I was in bed expecting to meet eternal peace when a light came forth into the corner of my room and told me I must get up and be prepared for this evening. I was told that faith must prevail and that God needed me for this one last night. Hear my words that come from Someone much greater than me. It is through faith and faith alone that we will come through this and all other trials that are laid before us. But it is my job to remind you tonight that God's building must be rebuilt, and that the same faith must exist inside the new walls as that which existed before—the only exception being that we not hide ourselves as we have done for so long."

The people began to cheer, and the roar of support was much louder than I would have expected—at least until I turned around and found that there were hundreds of people forming a large crowd behind me. I watched as an old gentleman, whom I recognized as Bart Farrow from the hardware store, stepped up to the front of the crowd and told the old lady that he could offer plumbing and electrical supplies, as well as an array of nails and screws needed for rebuilding. Then another man whom I also recognized came forward and pledged the lumber to build the new building. He was Jake Barton, owner of Barton's Lumberyard just outside of town. Then I watched as more men and then women stepped forward offering something, if only themselves, to the cause. I could feel my knees trembling, and I felt the sudden urge to pray. It wasn't unheard of for me to pray, but it certainly wasn't like me to want to do it in front of a crowd of people.

The crowd began to sing the old hymn "Bringing in the Sheaves," and people began to walk towards the old lady. I felt my feet guiding me up to the front behind others who were possibly being led as well. As I reached the front where now dozens of people were kneeling and I saw the preacher from town (*what was his name?*), I noticed that his skin was rough and aged. Then he leaned over my body as I knelt next to another gentleman, probably close to my age, and he whispered, "God could use you, Russ."

I felt a flood of tears roll from my eyes, and hard as I tried, I could not stop the roaring flow of emotions that was now flowing out of my body from the very depths of my soul. As I prayed to God that night, I knew that I could overcome all obstacles in my life, both great and small. I thanked God for His grace and mercy. I thanked Him for guiding me to that meeting, and I asked Him to let me be a big part of the church's reconstruction.

When I rose up from my kneeling position, I was shocked and confused as I saw no one else standing around. All of the cars were gone, and there were no people anywhere. I wondered how they could have left without my even hearing them, and yet I wasn't alarmed at all that I was standing out there all alone. The embers were still smoldering, and the red barn no longer existed. But I had a great story to write. I thought of how this could be the biggest story Locust Grove had ever had, and of how I would be the one who wrote about it!

I woke up early the next day so I could get a head start before anyone arrived at the office. The old barn story was going to be the biggest piece I had ever written, and I couldn't have Doris underfoot while I tried to get it out in an article. I drove to work that morning taking the route where the old barn had stood. I looked out of my car window as I passed the old barn which was now nothing more than a heap of smoldering ashes, and yet I knew that that heap of rubble was just the beginning of something new both to this town and to me personally. I wanted to do my part in helping to erect a new church on the old barn property. I wondered solemnly what that might be.

I arrived at the old brick building with the freshly painted white sign announcing in big bold black letters LOCUST GROVE REVIEW. The building was aligned next to several more that looked almost identical to it except for their own personalized signs overhead. My steps were hastily taken as I walked to the old wooden door with the double glass pane window centered at the top. I inserted my key and pushed the door open.

The musty smell of an old building greeted me as I turned on the office's only light in the front room. I felt my foot swiftly kick something that went gliding smoothly across the floor. As I looked down on the floor, I saw a big yellow envelope with *ATTENTION: Russell Banks* written in block letters on the outside. It was lying next to the old tin trashcan where it had come to a gliding stop. I stooped to pick it up and soon realized that my big story might not turn out to be very big after all.

I pulled out the collection of papers from the envelope and looked through them. The first was a picture of a young woman who looked familiar to me, and yet I could not place ever having met her. The paper beneath it was a hand-written note:

October 3, 1980

"Mr. Banks,

I am leaving this information for you because Locust Grove has lost one of its greatest citizens as of yesterday afternoon, and the county would want to know of this great loss. Miss Eloise F. Armstrong passed this life around one o'clock yesterday afternoon. She was born on December 6, 1875, and was the oldest living citizen in this community. She was instrumental in helping her father build a little church on the outskirts of town directly where the old barn that burned down yesterday had stood.

Her father was hanged when a band of travelers came riding through town and stopped in the church, behaving rowdily and drinking the devil's curse. They were asked to honor the church by leaving or to toss their bottles of moonshine from the premises. The ungodly trio attacked Preacher Fitchett, and then carried him to an old oak tree by Stevenson's mill and hung him there. Later that same evening, the church was burned to the ground. No one is certain who built the old barn, but rumor has it that the saints of God had instructed followers of Zacharias Fitchett to put it up secretly to discourage any more bandits from destroying it.

Eloise Armstrong was married briefly to a gentleman from Wolverton. He was a soldier during World War I and was killed in action about six months after their wedding. You can find more information on him if you need to at the Wolverton Library. I hear they have a nice article locating system over there.

I have enclosed some pictures of her, and I hope that you will do her justice in her obituary.

Thank you,

Someone who cared

I sat down in the swivel chair that Doris sat at each morning to answer the phone and do her secretarial duties, and I sifted through the collection of pictures that had been addressed to me. There was an identical copy in a smaller version of the black and white picture that was on top, and I felt again that I recognized her from somewhere. The next picture showed the young woman standing in front of an old church with an older gentleman that I guessed to be her father. It was something about that picture that made me pause and stare into it, and then it occurred to me: That was the church I had seen in my camera last night! It was exactly like it—right down to the small cast iron bell that was nailed to the right side by the front door, the same type if not the same bell that my friend Tommy and I had tossed rocks at as children on the way to school. This could not all be a coincidence, could it?

The bell at the top of the steeple was gleaming. It cast a reflection of sunbeams below, right on top of the man's head as though it were a halo of some sort. My heart began to race, and the paper in my hand was vibrating up and down displaying the condition my nerves were in. *How had I seen this church from my camera lens when it had been gone for years?*

The last picture seemed to help put some things into perspective for me. It was the portrait of an older lady, most likely in her fifties. She was obviously the lady I had seen the night before speaking to the crowd that had gathered in front of the barn. My heart did a little flip from within. If this were the lady I had seen last night, then there would not be much to my big story. She had already been dead or was dying when the old barn ignited. There was no way anyone would believe my story. Then it occurred to me that the men I had recognized the night before were all deceased as well. I had written their obituaries. Even the town preacher who had baptized me when I was a teen had gone on over to the other side, and yet I had seen him. I knew at that moment that God intended to use me. I didn't know what His purpose was then, but I am glad to say I do now.

I sat down at my typewriter in the back room that was damp from being sealed overnight, and I plucked out on my computer, FIRE DESTROYS OLD BARN. And I proceeded to write another boring story on another boring fire. At the bottom of the article, I did make a small exception to the usual article. I stated that suggestions had been made to build a new church where the old barn had stood, and I asked anyone who was interested to show up on the following Saturday to make preparations for it.

Much to my surprise, I found the entire town congregated around the lot where the old barn had stood. Some were in trucks with business labels on the sides and supplies spilling over the tops of their truck beds. After some brief planning, we had that church built in less than ninety days! Out front we erected a huge cross that we engraved with this message, "This church built in memory of Eloise F. Armstrong, a faithful follower who served God right up until her calling. May she rest in peace." I sighed as I read it because I knew that she had served Him even beyond her calling in some magical way that is beyond explanation.

I wrote up the finest obituary I could to help the townspeople fully understand the role Eloise Armstrong had played in keeping her father's church alive long after his death. The private meetings did not need to go on for thirty-some odd years in secrecy. Eloise would have been safe to open up the church doors again for the world. At her departure, she had realized the one thing that she had done wrong in her walk of faith. She had kept it quiet and not spread it all around. I wonder if God gave her a chance to really change things or if He just used me to accomplish it. Regardless, I like the way He handled things.

Several days after the barn fire, I picked up the developed film that I had taken there. I wasn't surprised to find that they were of the barn and of the firemen working to put out its roaring flames. Interesting enough, though, the last picture was that of a new white church with beautiful flowers and shrubs all around it. And naturally, on the right hand-side of the door was the old cast iron dinner bell.

As for the cast iron bell, it was found among the ashes of the barn. I personally took it home, cleaned it, and painted it. Then I brought it to the new church and placed it on the front right side of the door. I used the photograph I had gotten with the film from the burning barn to make a floor plan for our new church. I did the same for the landscaping. It's funny to me how I managed to get hold of a picture of the church before it was ever built.

I still haven't learned all the history of the lot that the new church sits upon, but I know enough to know that saints have walked upon those grounds.

ACTS 2:46-47: And they, continuing daily with one accord in the temple, and breaking bread from house to house, did eat their meat with gladness and singleness of heart, praising God, and having favour with all the people. And the Lord added to the church daily such as should be saved.

Raggedy Annie

Snow fell softly on my face as the chill of the morning air stung my cheeks. My lungs drew in an icy flood of cold air that chilled me from within. The day was silent, and I could almost hear the snowflakes falling softly on the road, and just beginning to stick to it. I marveled at all the beauty that surrounded me. The pine trees that stretched up into the sky were layered in white sheets of glistening snow that had fallen several days earlier. The cornfields were covered in white, and I had to squint my eyes at the brightness of the whole scene. It was a true scene of tranquility.

Everything seemed as it should be as I stood looking at the fields surrounded by snow-blanketed trees. As I took in the enchanting sight before me, I noticed an opening in the woods across the corn-field. From where I was standing, I could see a large deer in the rays of the sun there in the opening, and he was gazing at me. His large antlers had a number of huge points, and he looked as big as a moose.

I watched as the huge animal shook his head at me. It was as though he was calling me over towards him. I stared in disbelief as I watched him do it again and again. I know it sounds like I'm coming from way out there, but I was certain that the monstrous beast in the woods was calling me in the only way he knew how to.

I looked back at my house and saw that the chimney was sending its puff of smoke from the brick chute at the top. I thought to myself that there was nothing pressing at home that would require me to be back right away. The weather was perfect for a short walk, anyway, and with that I turned towards the cornfield and started walking toward the opening.

My first obstacle was a trench that had been built around the field to help drain it during wet spells, and that did turn out to be quite an obstacle. It wasn't a big trench; in fact, I even found a place where it was hardly a step across. It was the black sticky mud that was waiting on the other side for me that messed me up. I had just stepped from the roadside of the ditch onto the field side when I began to make my way up the ditch and my foot refused to move. There was this fighting hold it had on the bottom of my shoe that was keeping me from bringing my blue rubber snow boot out of the marsh-like substance. I jerked my foot as hard as I could to dislodge it from the clutch that the black ooze had on me. When I felt my body go toppling right into the ditch, I prepared for landing. The briars and twigs that are usually lingering about in the ditch were blanketed in snow, so I was protected from them. It was the fall that brought forth a piercing throb to my wrist and ankle. I had somehow managed to topple in on my right side. My right wrist had tried to catch me, and my right foot was still twisted and stuck in the black mud. As I lay there in the ditch to catch my breath, I felt my foot gently pop free from the clutches of the earth sending, a loud sucking noise into the day's silent atmosphere.

I stood up and brushed the snow and mud off of my waterproof sweat suit I had put on over my jeans. I was deciding on forgetting about the opening on the other side of the field when I looked up and saw the deer again. This time it had reared its huge head from out of the forest line and was standing in the full sun. It was still gesturing his head in *that way* that looked as though it was calling me. I wasn't feeling very good about it, but I knew that I would not rest if I did not go towards that overgrown beast in the woods. *Okay,* I said under my breath, *I've come this far; what more do I have to lose?* and I headed across the snow-blanketed field that looked almost heavenly from where I stood.

I could hear the sucking sounds coming from each footstep as I pulled my rubbers from out of the soft earth below my feet. I wondered how the deer tracks had made it across so graciously and without much evidence of disturbing the earth below the snow when I was leaving behind a trail of snow and mud that took away greatly from the field's beauty. The muscles in my legs began to ache from the constant pulling I was doing to my legs as I physically struggled with each footstep I tried to take. My breath was running short, and the tip of my nose was cold from the wind that swept across the field.

The deer had backed up again into the trail and was standing there below the only light in the opening. He didn't move. I stepped into the opening slowly and stared at the huge beast. I gazed straight into his dark brown eyes, and he began to move his head once more as if telling me that I had not gone far enough and we must continue on. Then he sprinted into the woods as quickly as one would expect a deer to do that had just been approached by a human being, and he was gone. Why did I feel as though this simple animal thought I would follow him? It all seemed a bit crazy, yet there was something logical about me following that deer that seemed to be calling me for some reason I had yet to discover.

I looked behind me through the opening and stared across the field that now bore my muddy footprints across its terrain. It seemed like a long way to walk for nothing, so I shrugged my shoulders and followed the prints of the unusual animal I had encountered. The trees were all covered in snow that was beginning to melt, and I could hear the soft dripping of water as it fell from the trees. I saw a turkey buzzard fly over and dip down ahead as though it had found a possible meal. I wondered if that deer was trying to guide me back to his mate. I thought that perhaps some wandering hunter could have shot his mate, and he was now desperate enough to help out his love by calling on a human being. *That sounds ridiculous,* I thought to myself. But wouldn't having a deer wave his head at you seem a bit ridiculous, too?

It didn't matter to me now whether the deer was calling me or just rousing my curiosity I was on the wooded side of the field for the first time since I had moved to Burgess, and I was going to take a look around. I began to follow the hoof prints that led straight down the trail as far as I could see. There was no sign of the curious deer. He was nowhere in sight. I didn't really mind that the deer had left because I was actually enjoying the fresh air and beautiful scenery that was glistening with snow all around me. Peace could be found back here where there was no sign of man and his modern technology. I marveled at how perfectly the creator had made everything around me. No debris was lying around this wooded place, and nature was at its best. There were no twigs to pull out of my way, nor spider webs to run into this time of the year. That in itself was a blessing. I'm the type to coil up like one of those roly-poly bugs you find under rotten wood when I see a spider, and a direct encounter with its web could send me into spasms of true anxiety.

I began to notice that the trail was getting much smaller and the woods were becoming thicker when I saw something lying under one of the huge trees in front of me. It was red and white, and it seemed to have some sort of orange yarn attached to it. I walked towards the tree trying to figure out what the object was before reaching it. I approached the object and bent down to wipe the snow from off of its surface. Then I grew curious as to why I might find an old Raggedy Anne doll so far away from civilization. I wiped the snow from her face and hair, and I realized that this doll had not been out here long. That seemed impossible since the woods were so far away from any houses. The nearest was mine and that was now close to two miles away.

I looked around past the tree to see if I could find something that might suggest why this doll was here, and I saw nothing. I sat down on a tree that had fallen over and was now offering seating for tired travelers (at least in this case), and I inspected the doll. It was just like many of the other Raggedy Anne dolls you might find at any local department store, but I hadn't seen one in a while. Then I saw the writing on the tag that stuck out from the side of the doll's torso. *Annie Barnes* was hand-written in tiny print on the back of the label that said "MADE IN JAPAN." It was then that I felt a warm rush of blood run through my chilled body.

Annie Barnes's photograph had been on every local news network around. Her mother had awakened yesterday to find Annie gone from her room. The police had been calling it a possible kidnapping and were checking the files of all sex offenders. For a moment I entertained the idea that I should return home and call the police. Then I decided that I had to look around a little longer. She could be freezing to death. And if I found nothing, I would call the police and tell them that I had found her doll and the location where I found it. I looked up in the sky and said a little prayer before rising up off of my ready-made chair in the forest: "Dear God, If that little girl is all right, please guide and direct me to her. If that child's body is lying around here, please show me so I can take it home to the people who loved her. And dear God, please give me the strength to deal with whatever it is that I encounter today. Amen."

I was scared, and there's no getting around that. I'm not the type of person who would take on such a task as this on my own, but I hadn't had much choice under the circumstances. I had a feeling now that little Annie Barnes would be out in this wooded area, and I was afraid that the brisk chill that had filled the air the night before might have killed her. Even if that was to be the case, I had it in my heart to locate the child and bring her to a final resting spot—to a place where the people who loved her could mourn and say good-by to her. I continued on in the direction that I had been going when I found the doll, and I looked around for the deer prints in the snow. Perhaps that huge beast knew where I would find the little girl and was trying to let me know in the only way that it could. I let my feet take me along the trail of hoof prints that did not disturb the earth below the snow.

The trail ended about thirty feet ahead of the location of the doll. I had wanted to turn back and yet couldn't. There was something driving me to walk through this wooded area that was getting even denser with each step I took, and then I heard it. It was a soft whimpering that could have easily been mistaken for an ailing bird or some small creature from the forest. Yet I had a feeling that the whimpering was that of a human being, and with the grace of God that human being would be little Annie Barnes.

I stopped and held my breath in the cold air hoping to hear in which direction the sounds were coming from. It was up ahead, and I was more certain than ever that it was a child's cries that I was hearing. I continued on my path until I saw a large bundle of branches with thorns stacked in a very thick pile. It spread practically the entire length of the area before me. It appeared as though some type of wild animal had built it to protect itself from the hardships of nature. I drew nearer to it to inspect how difficult it might be to cross over it.

The thorns on the wiry branches were the biggest I had ever seen. I thought that those natural weapons could surely cut somebody up pretty badly. Whatever animal had built this place was certainly protecting itself from something, practically everything.

I could hear the cries on the other side of this animal shelter, and they were becoming a little audible. "Waggian. Waggian." is what I could hear the voice calling out. I looked around me to see if there was a way over the huge mass of thorns. There had to be some way of protecting myself from those miniature swords waiting to slice open my skin. I looked down the length of the thorny mess in front of me, and there I saw it. If I had been looking too quickly, I would surely have missed it. The opening to the mass of thorns was blocked by a mountain laurel bush, and it was radiating a beauty around the white snowy background that made me gasp in awe. The buds were beginning to open, and they were displaying a beautiful array of red-dish pink blooms that only mesmerized the naked eye.

'Waggedy! Waggedy!' I heard the small voice cry, bringing me back to what was now my purpose of this venture.

"I'm coming!" I heard myself say as I dropped to my knees to crawl under the bush of beauty that stood before me. I could feel the thorns grabbing hold of my skin as I tried to slip through the open-ing that I had discovered behind the evergreen bush, and my wrist pounded each time I moved forward on it. "Hold on, Sweety! I'll be there very soon!" I could feel this desperation sweeping over me as if every second mattered.

I heard the jacket of my water proof sweatsuit let out a ripping sound that suggested it might not be much use after this excursion, but it seemed to matter little to me at that moment. I had to get to the child who was sobbing for help somewhere behind the jungle of thorns in front of me. The opening became wider, and I could see a little girl with golden curls huddled in a corner of this vast shelter in the middle of nowhere. And then I saw her tiny face.

Her cheeks were rosy from the cold air that had obviously been surrounding her for many hours. Her red and white striped pajamas were ripped and tattered, and she looked like a real life Raggedy Anne. And yet there was the most beautiful smile on her face that beamed through tears when she saw me.

"Waggian!" she exclaimed as she jumped up from the spot where she had sought shelter from the weather and ran to me, her arms outstretched.

I held my arms out to her so she could run into them, but she stopped at my hands and took the doll that I had forgotten I was holding and said once again, "Waggian!"

"Yes! Raggedy Anne," I said back to her.

I quickly inspected the little girl I had found in the woods and thought that it would be fine if we traveled on out of the forest. She was missing one of her candy striped bedroom slippers, and her toes looked blue from the cold air. There were some scratches on her face and arms, but she looked in pretty good shape under the circumstances. I took off the athletic jacket I had put on over my wool coat and removed it. I wrapped little Annie Barnes in my coat as best I could, put on my jacket, and picked up the child, resting her on my hip as I prepared for the long walk back.

I looked around the shelter of thorns and wondered how I would get out of the web of tiny swords without scratching the little girl when I saw the buck that had led me to this child. He nodded his head once more and walked through some light brush that I would have never found for myself. I proceeded after him, but I did not see him anywhere on the trail he had directed me to. He left me directions in the snow, however. His hoof prints led me out of the forest right behind my own house. I could see the smoke rising from the chimney, and my feet began to run towards the warmth that was awaiting me and the little Raggedy Annie I had on my hip.

As I walked in the door, I immediately called the police and let them know I had found the precious little girl. As I looked for an old sweatshirt to cover her small body with, I could hear the sirens making their way to my home. The child I had found in raggedy clothing beneath a thicket was safe, and there were some people waiting for her, and they were going to be very happy about that.

Much happened after that. The rescue people showed up to examine her, her parents arrived, and even the media came out that day. There was so much publicity over the loss of the child that everyone wanted to know the details of the child's location. I am not one who enjoys standing before cameras, so I simply said that she had been found in the woods. I told the police, though, about the deer and following the prints. I was hoping someone would believe my remarkable experience. They didn't seem to be as impressed with my story as I was.

When Raggedy Annie's mother walked up to her and embraced her, she asked her little tot through the squeeze, "Where have you been, Precious?"

The child looked at her doll and softly said, "With Waggedy." We all laughed at her innocence of all that had happened to her.

The day wore down, and everything had gone back to the ordinary when an officer knocked on my front door. I was preparing a roast in the kitchen and feeling rushed, so when I opened the door I was afraid I had offended him because he seemed confused as I guided the storm door open.

"Sorry to bother you, ma'am," he said as he tipped his hat, "but I have some discrepancies to your story. We followed your footprints out to the field and into the forest, and everything is almost like you said. There's just one thing."

"Well, what is that?" I asked as I wiped my hands with a kitchen towel.

"We saw no indication of deer prints anywhere. There is not even a footprint of the little girl around—just some flat marks that suggest something was dragged into the thicket where you found her huddling. I don't know about you, ma'am, but I'm not going to say too much about this. I believe you had some kind of supernatural *something,* but I don't think too many others might believe it. You have a good evening ma'am," he said as he tipped his hat once more and turned to walk back to his car that was waiting for him in the driveway.

There were many unanswered questions that day, like how did Annie get from her house five miles away to a location so far from everything? And why did Annie's parents get back together after her disappearance? And what led them to church that morning to give their lives to Christ? And there are even more disturbing ones, like how could a deer communicate to a human being? And how could a child exist at night in twenty-degree temperatures without anything to keep her warm? I may never know, but I'll bet if ran into that deer again he could tell me the answers. Why not? It wouldn't be the first time that God has used an animal.

Curiously, just last summer my husband and I were cleaning the woods behind our home. While pulling some thick thorny branches from a pile, we discovered Raggedy Annie's missing slipper. I'm not going to give you any ideas about what it was doing out there, but isn't it interesting?

Numbers 2:28: *And the Lord opened the mouth of the ass, and she said unto Ba'laam, What have I done unto thee, that thou hast smitten me three times?*

0-595-25656-2